SOME SWEET DAY

SOME SWEET DAY

BY BRYAN WOOLLEY

 RANDOM HOUSE · NEW YORK

Copyright © 1973 by Bryan Woolley
All rights reserved under International and Pan American
Copyright Conventions. Published in the United States by
Random House, Inc., New York, and simultaneously in Canada
by Random House of Canada Limited, Toronto.

Library of Congress Cataloging in Publication Data
Woolley, Bryan.
Some sweet day.
I. Title.
PZ4.W918So [PS3573.067]   813'.5'4   73-13701
ISBN 0-394-48714-1

Manufactured in the United States of America
98765432
First Edition

TO PEGGY

SOME SWEET DAY

MOTES of dust swam in the yellow shaft of late sunlight. I was trying to focus on just one of them while it was still up near the window and follow it all the way down to the piece of tin where we set up the stove in winter. Nero, lying outside the screen door, raised her head from between her paws and pricked her ears toward the barn.

I heard his singing too.

There'll be smoke on the mountain, on the land and
*   the sea,*
When the Army and Navy overtake the en-e-mee . . .

A song we heard sometimes when the radio batteries were charged and we could pick something out of the static.

He stopped at the horse trough, scooped up water in his yellow straw hat and held it over his head to let the water filter through onto his hair. The first drops rolled down without penetrating his black mane, divided into little streams at the nape of his neck, then ran quickly down his bare brown shoulders and disappeared under his overalls. He said "Ahhh!" then laid his hat and glasses on the trough's rock rim and washed his face, snorting in the green water. Then he replaced his hat and glasses and reached toward the fence. I hadn't seen his shotgun propped there. He cradled it lovingly as he strode across the dusty barnyard, his long, vague shadow fleeing before him.

Nero rose, wagging lazily, and greeted him at the yard gate. He climbed the porch steps, dropped the gun to his side and peered through the screen, his right hand holding the sun away from his eyes.

"Gate, get your hat and come," he said.

He had already headed back across the barnyard by the time I opened the door to follow him. Nero plodded along beside him, panting. I ran to catch up, and asked, "Where we going?"

"Just to bring the cows up," he said. "Thought I'd take you along in case I found sign of something. You could bring the cows on in."

I strutted beside him, proud that he thought I could do such a job, and watched him open the pasture gate. He was fine to look upon. His long black hair leaked from under his hat. Water still seeped from under the sweatband, and a drop or two clung to his sideburns. His tall, slender frame was slightly stooped, making his blue overalls appear to fit more snugly in back than in front.

"You know what, Daddy?" I said to his back.

"What?"

"When I get big, I want to be just like you."

He laughed. "I ain't much."

"I want to be a farmer like you, and drive a tractor like you, and wear glasses like you, and have a gun like you, and have a dog like Nero . . ."

"Nero ain't much, either. I'd have shot her a long time ago if she hadn't bit the preacher. That's why I called her Nero. He didn't like Baptists, either. It's hard to shoot a dog like that."

"You called Nero after a *man*?"

"Yeah. An old-timey king."

We walked quietly through the junipers, Daddy's eyes scanning the ground on each side of the cow path, Nero dashing back and forth, sniffing things, chasing birds.

"Daddy, can I shoot your gun?"

"No."

"Just once?"

"Six years old is too little to be going around shooting guns. It'd knock you on your ass."

"Joe George's daddy lets him shoot *his* gun."

"Who says?"

"Joe George."

"Joe George is a liar."

He stopped abruptly, raised the gun and fired into a large oak. A dark ball crashed through the leaves to the ground.

"Go get him, Gate. Stay here, Nero!"

The squirrel's eyes were open. "I don't think it's dead yet," I said.

"It's dead. Pick it up."

I didn't want to, but I did. It was soft and warm and lay limp across my hand like a newborn puppy. I tried to keep my hand away from the wet places where the shot went in, but there were too many of them, and I could feel a warm dampness on my hand. It was the first time I'd ever held anything dead. I carried it to Daddy and tried to hand it to him. "You carry him," he said.

We found the cows over near the bluff and headed them back along the path toward the barn. The sun was going down ahead of us, and the sky was afire with red and purple and orange and yellow and green. All that color and light and the soft scratch of the cows' hooves on the hard path and the warm cow smell and the sound of Nero's panting as she worried the cows along their way and the feel of Daddy being close was almost more than I could stand. I wanted to just unzip my hide and cram it all inside of me to keep forever. I even forgot the dead squirrel I was carrying along by the tail now. The tail, which looked so thick and pretty, was really very skinny under its long hair, almost like a rat's.

"Boy, everything sure looks fine, doesn't it, Daddy?"

"Yeah. God sure was stupid to make people when he could have kept all this for himself."

When we passed the gate, the cows made a beeline for the milk pen, and Daddy went on ahead of me to pitch them some hay. Nero wandered after him, and I stopped to close the gate.

"Gate!" Daddy yelled at me over the milk-pen fence. "Take that squirrel to the house and tell your ma to fix it for supper. Then come on back and get the eggs."

I broke into a trot, but stopped when I got to the sleeping porch door. Rick was still asleep. He and Belinda both had the measles, handed on from me on the last day of school. I tiptoed across into the kitchen. Mother was sitting at the table, kind of lying there, actually, with her head on her arms. She didn't look up.

"Mother?"

"Hmm? Where's Daddy?"

"Milking. Belinda asleep, too?"

"Finally. I'll sure be glad when this siege is over with."

"Me and Daddy killed a squirrel." I laid it on the table beside her. Its eyes were still open, but somehow it looked deader, as if it never really had been alive. "He wants it for supper."

She raised her head and started to say something, but she just looked at me for a long time, then kind of smiled. "Sure wish he'd skinned it first."

"I've got to go get the eggs."

"The bucket's on the sleeping porch."

"I'll just use my hat."

I heard Daddy cussing before I got back to the barn, so I knew he was through with Blossom and had started on Bess. "Saw, Bess! Saw, you son of a bitch!" he said. Bess always kicked.

The hens were already on their roost, scratching around, trying to get comfortable, quarreling quietly with each other. The nests were lined along one wall of the henhouse, like a row of big post office boxes with straw. I plunged my hand into the one nearest the door and felt in the straw, finding only sticky broken eggshells. That damned Nero! She had been through the whole row. Only three good eggs in the whole house. I put them in my hat and went out to the milk pen to sit on the top rail and watch Daddy.

"How many?"

"Three. Looks like Nero's been sucking them again. Nothing but a bunch of broken shells in there."

"God damn it!" He pulled one of Bess' tits too hard. She jerked to one side and kicked over the milk bucket. The milk fanned out over the ground. "God damn! God damn! God damn!" Daddy kicked the milk bucket. It wobbled across the pen like a crazy top and clanged into the fence. "God damn!" He kicked Bess as hard as he could right in the belly. She grunted, sidled away from him, and trotted slowly over to the corner where Blossom was chewing her hay. Daddy stood in the middle of the pen, his fists clenched tight, breathing hard. It was almost dark now, and I could barely make out his face. I sat as quietly as I could, holding the eggs in my hat. Nero stood panting. He saw her. "Gate," he said, "bring me my quirt."

I eased off the fence as quickly as I could without dropping the eggs and opened the door to the feed room, where Daddy's quirt hung on a nail. "Here, Nero!" Daddy called. "Come on here to Daddy!" Nero wagged like crazy and romped up to him. Daddy grabbed her collar and walked her through the gate and around toward the henhouse. I followed, carrying the quirt and my hat with the eggs. Nero began to realize what was about to happen. She tucked her tail between her legs and braced her feet against the ground. Daddy just dragged her along as if he didn't notice her resistance. He unlatched the henhouse door and after we all went in, he closed it. He held out his free hand, and I put the quirt in it, and he started whaling the tar out of poor Nero. She jumped around and yelped and squealed at the top of her voice, but Daddy just kept laying the leather on her. The chickens were all awake and flying and flopping, squawking to high heaven. Feathers drifted down around me. I couldn't see anything, it was so dark. I wanted to put my hands over my ears, but I didn't know what to do with the eggs. And I was afraid one of those crazy chickens was going to fly right into my face.

Finally, Daddy stopped. He opened the door a crack and Nero took off toward the house, whimpering all the way. We went back to the milk pen, and Daddy hung up the quirt, picked up his shotgun and the empty milk bucket, and we headed for the house. Daddy was real quiet now, and I wasn't about to say anything, either. About halfway to the house, I stubbed my toe on the water pipe that went to the horse trough. The three eggs flew out of my hat, and I fell flat on my face. I wasn't wearing shoes, and my big toe hurt like crazy. The gravel cut into my knees and elbows, and I tasted dirt and chicken shit in my mouth. I was winded, and I felt tears burning in my eyes. I couldn't get up. Daddy just stood there a minute, then he said quietly, "Get up, son." I finally worked my way back up to my feet, and just as I was standing steady, Daddy gave me a hard kick right in the ass, and I went sprawling again. I really cried this time. Daddy just stood there. After a while he said again, "Get up, son." I just couldn't make it all the way this time, so he shifted the milk bucket over to his gun hand and grabbed my arm and lifted me. He reached down and handed me my hat. "You've just got to be more careful, son," he said softly.

Mother was waiting for us at the fence. She had lighted the lamp in the kitchen, and I could see her standing there against the light through my tears. "What on earth's been going on out there?" she asked, worry in her voice. "I never *heard* such a racket!"

"Nothing to worry about," Daddy said. "We've just got no milk to drink, no eggs to eat, a cow that kicks, a dog that sucks eggs, and a boy that falls all over himself. We're doing fine! Just fine!" He dropped the milk bucket by the gate and walked around the house to the front porch. Rick let out a squawk, and Mother rushed inside to tend to him before he woke Belinda. I sat down under the windmill to rest and check over my wounds. Rick stopped crying, so I knew Mother was rocking him.

Pretty soon, I heard Harley May's dogs baying beyond the bluff. It was a peaceful sound and it almost took my mind away from my stinging scratches and throbbing toe and tailbone. After a while, I looked up and saw Daddy standing by the gate, looking at me. I felt the hairs stand up on the back of my neck. I hadn't heard him come around the house. The shotgun, cradled in his arms, caught the light from the kitchen. He spoke to me softly through the darkness. "Tell your mother I've saddled Old Blue and gone to find Harley." He disappeared toward the barn, and soon I heard Old Blue's hooves on the gravel and the squeak of Daddy's saddle as he climbed down to open the pasture gate.

I didn't go in until I heard the squirrel sizzling in the frying pan.

The morning was bright, and outside the screen Nero lapped from the bowl under the leaky faucet in the yard. She looked all right. She probably didn't even remember last night. The house was quiet. I could hear Mother moving in the kitchen, but that was all. Rick's bed was empty. My knees and elbows still felt raw, and my toe and my tailbone were sore. I knew I was going to hurt like hell when I tried to get up.

Mother came to the door. When she saw that I was awake, she held out a piece of sausage in a biscuit. She looked down at me silently for a long while, and I looked back silently.

"How you feeling?" she asked finally.

"Okay, I guess."

"Can you sit up?"

"I don't know."

"Here, I'll help you."

She placed her arm behind my neck and lifted me. My tailbone hurt during the bend, but felt better after I was sitting up. She handed me the biscuit and sausage, and I ate it while she examined my knees and elbows. They weren't pretty, especially with all that Mercurochrome she put on them last night. She untied the turpentine-soaked rag and unwrapped my toe. "Not too bad," she said, "but you split the nail. You'll be barefooted when Gran comes tonight, but I guess you would have been, anyway."

"Where's Daddy?"

"Still asleep. He didn't get in till daylight."

"Did him and Harley get anything?"

"One fox."

"Where's Belinda and Rick?"

"On a pallet in the living room. They're better. Can you get all the way up?"

I got to my feet, and she pulled down my drawers and looked at my tailbone. "You've got a good one, all right. Nice and blue. Think you can walk okay?"

"I guess."

"Well, get dressed then, and go outside. Stay away from the house for a while. When I'm ready for you to come back, I'll hang the ice blanket on the clothesline. Okay?"

"Why do you want me to do that?"

"Just hush and do what I say."

She helped me on with my clothes, and I hobbled outside. The milk bucket still lay by the gate. The milk pen was empty, so I knew that Mother had let the cows out to pasture. The sun was bright and warm and felt good on me. I crawled through the fence behind the barn, and Nero slid under the bottom wire and tagged along with me. A turkey gobbled somewhere over to the north as I walked toward the bluff.

About halfway up the side, before it really gets steep, there's a large oak with a big flat rock under it. I sat down on the rock, and Nero plopped down beside me and laid her head between her paws. She looked at me out of the corner of her eye, and I ran my hand up and down her old black-and-white-spotted hide and then rubbed her behind the ears. She closed her eyes and sighed.

I could see home very well from my rock. Below me were the big old barn, and the corn crib, and the tractor shed, and the house with its rock chimney— all gray, wooden, worn-out-looking buildings that nestled close to the darker earth. They gleamed cleanly in the morning sun. For a while it looked as if nothing was moving in the whole world except my hand behind Nero's ears and those silly white chickens in the barnyard. I wondered how they felt after all their squawking and fluttering last night.

The front porch screen opened and shut. A second later, I heard the rifle-crack of its closing. Daddy sat down on the steps. He held something, and soon I knew it was his fiddle. Nero heard it, too. She opened her eyes and jerked her head up and lifted her ears. She listened a moment, then dropped her head and closed her eyes again, and I went on rubbing her.

Daddy always went out on the porch when he wanted to fiddle. He never let any of us go out with him. We could hear the music in the house, he said, and he didn't want us standing around watching him. He was playing longer than usual this morning. He played slow for a while, then fast for a while. And then he sat and looked down the lane for a long time. Then he played some more. I just sat on my rock and rubbed Nero's ears and listened. A long time later, Daddy rose and went into the house. In a little while he came back out, got into the car and drove down the lane. He slowed at the corner by the mailbox, then turned into the road to Darlington and disappeared over a hill. Just then, Mother walked into the yard with the red ice blanket and hung it on the clothesline.

He returned in time to milk looking happy. He was sitting on the steps, bouncing Rick on his knee when Gran arrived. Nero, barking and leaping, met her at the gate. Gran jumped back. "Down! Down! Get away from here!"

Daddy grinned. "Don't let the dog scare you, Gloria. She won't bite."

"She was about to ruin my hose. Hose don't grow on trees these days, you know. Where's Lacy?"

"In the kitchen. Supper's waiting. You going to spend the night?"

"If I don't get eaten by this dog first, I am."

"How are things in town?"

Gran glared at him through her steel-rimmed glasses. "I thought you'd know. I heard you were there today." She stamped into the house and slammed the screen. Daddy got up, swinging Rick out and above his head.

The plates and the oilcloth shone in the light of the lamp, surrounded by chicken and dumplings and green beans and biscuits. Belinda and Rick argued, as they always did, over who would sit by Gran, and Daddy settled it, as he always did, putting one on each side of her. Everybody was hungry, and we ate quietly, Mother smiling at our appetites and our compliments.

Gran usually led the supper conversation when she drove from Darlington to visit us. In the fall, she talked of school and how her fifth-graders were doing. In the spring and summer, she talked of revivals and baptisms. And always of what was going on in town— who was home on furlough, who had been killed, what the Fort Worth *Star-Telegram* said about the Japs and the Germans, Roosevelt and Churchill. But tonight she was silent, and Daddy was aware of her gaze from across the table. Mother saw it, too, and was fidgety.

Finally, Gran asked, "Has Will told you about his trip to town, Lacy?"

"A little," she replied. "I don't guess there's much to tell."

"I understand he had a lot of business to conduct at the drugstore. Or was it upstairs *over* the drugstore, Will?"

Mother's chair scraped the floor. "I'd better start washing these," she said. "Ricky, Gate, Belinda, get out of here. You've dawdled with your food long enough."

Everybody except Daddy got up, and Mother started talking to Gran about a dress she was making. She rattled the dishes into the sink. I asked her to punch some holes in the lid of a fruit jar for me, and Belinda, Rick and I went out by the windmill to catch lightning bugs. Daddy was still sitting at the table, smoking a cigarette, saying nothing.

The breeze was up, and we could hear the windmill whirring slowly in the gloom above us. We stood still

and watched. Soon Belinda said, "Look! There's one!"
I handed her the jar and told her to take the lid off.
I sneaked up on the little light that was blinking
under the windmill. It flitted lazily here and there,
and I followed it, my hands cupped, ready. Then I
reached, clapped my hands together, and felt the
tickle inside.

"I got it! Bring the jar!"

Belinda was there, and quickly clapped the lid on
when I dropped the bug in. "Look, Rick," she said,
holding it out for him to see. The bug was crawling
around the bottom, blinking his tail on and off.

"Ooooh! Pretty!" Rick exclaimed. He laughed and
jumped up and down.

I caught more, and Belinda added them to our collection, Rick laughing and squealing after each new
capture. After a while, I got tired of running after
the things, and we sat down under the windmill to
watch the ones we'd got and wonder what made them
blink like that. Belinda and Rick seemed small and
warm, and I reached out and put a hand on each head
and messed up their soft hair. We all giggled. Then
we heard the sink water splattering on the ground
under the house, and knew that Mother and Gran
had finished the dishes. Mother came to the door.

"Rick, Belinda, come in now. Time for bed."

"Aw, Mother," Belinda whined.

"You've been sick and need your rest. Come on,
now."

They wandered slowly up the steps. I sat a while
longer, watching the bugs in the jar and the still-
uncaptured ones blinking here and there around the
windmill. I wondered if my prisoners were signaling

to their comrades, urging rescue. Then I heard Mother
tell Rick to potty, and I knew he was ready for bed.
I picked up the jar and went in too, and sat on the
edge of his bed. We watched the bugs blink off and
on, off and on. Mother and Gran were in the living
room. Gran spoke in low tones about the drugstore
and "Laverne Thomas, that hussy." Mother spoke
sometimes, too, but so quietly I couldn't make out
her words. Finally, I got up and handed the jar to
Rick. He shoved it under the sheet and pulled the
sheet over his head. I could see the little lights blinking through the cloth. I smiled and walked into the
kitchen.

Daddy startled me. I didn't expect to see him there,
still sitting at the table, still smoking a cigarette. He
watched me cross the room.

Mother knelt on the living room floor, pinning a
pattern to a piece of cloth. Gran was sitting, rocking,
watching her. They stopped talking when I came in.
I stood and watched Mother for a while, not knowing
what else to do. Mother's red hair shone in the light
of the lamp she had placed on the floor beside her.
She was pretty, bending there. A snip of her scissors
now and then and the creak of Gran's rocker in the
half-darkness were the only sounds in the house.

"Gran?" I spoke softly and didn't even know why.

"Huh?"

"Will you read me a story?"

"Okay. Get your book."

"No stories." Daddy's voice drifted in from the
kitchen.

"What?" Gran asked.

"No stories, I said."

"Why not, Will?"

"Because I said so. This is *my* house. If I say no stories under this roof tonight, there won't be any."

Mother had stopped pinning. Her eyes were closed. Gran raised her eyebrows and rocked faster. I heard Daddy get up and walk across the sleeping porch and slam the screen. I sat down on the floor and leaned against the wall. Mother started pinning again, and Gran rocked faster. It was so quiet I could hear the faucet dripping in the kitchen. After a while, Gran got up and said, "Come on, Gate."

She grabbed a couple of matches from the kitchen matchbox and stalked to the sleeping porch. Rick was asleep. She reached under his sheet and got the lightning-bug jar and put it on the floor. It was still blinking. Then she slid the cardboard box that I kept my books in out from under my bed, grabbed the top book, and slid the box back. She grabbed the lantern off the hook by the door, motioned for me to come, and marched out the door, down the steps, around the house, through the front gate, out to the tractor shed. She struck a match, lit the lantern, hung it on a nail, and handed me the book.

"Pick a story," she said.

I flipped through the book until I got to "The Wolf and the Fox" and handed it back. I climbed into the tractor seat. She sat down on a big can that Daddy kept old baling wire in and started reading.

"A wolf and a fox once lived together. The fox, who was the weaker of the two, had to do all the hard work, which made him anxious to leave his companion." She read fast and loud, like she was bawling out one of her pupils. "One day, passing through a wood, the wolf said, 'Red-fox, get me something to eat, or I shall eat you.'" She read on and on, never stopping to look at me, never making faces like the fox and the wolf or trying to talk like they would talk, as she usually did. I sat there on the tractor, moving the steering wheel back and forth, not liking the story very much, and wishing I was somewhere else.

Finally, she looked up at me, and I saw tears in her eyes behind her glasses. She wiped her eyes and kind of laughed. "I'm not reading this very well, am I?" she said.

"Not like you usually do. Why are you crying?"

"Nothing you should worry about, little one. Don't try to understand why grownups act the way they do. It'll just make you sad." She raised the book again.

"You don't have to finish it if you don't want to."

She smiled. "You know how it ends, don't you?"

"Yeah. The farmer beats the wolf to death."

She nodded. "And the fox?"

"He gets away."

"And lives happily ever after?"

We heard the gravel crunch and looked up, and Daddy stepped into the light. He stood there, looking at us, and we looked at him. Gran sighed and lifted her glasses and wiped her eyes again. Daddy walked over and took the book out of her lap and looked at it.

"I thought I said no stories."

"We're not in the house, Will."

He slammed her in the face with the book. The can rocked back, and Gran fell onto the gravel. Her glasses dropped off her nose, and she just lay there on the ground, sobbing. I started crying, too. I felt like something had busted inside of me, and the tears kept coming, and I thought I'd never be able to stop them. Finally, Gran got up and put her glasses on. One lens was cracked. She limped out of the shed into the darkness. I sat there on the tractor, bawling, and Daddy just stood there, holding the book. Then I heard Gran's car engine start, and I jumped down and ran past Daddy. The car was turning around, and the lights were on. She was leaving. I ran to catch her. She rolled the window down.

"Go back, Gate," she said. "You can't come."

"Stop! Please stop, Gran!"

"I've got to go, Gate! Go to your mother!" The car moved slowly down the lane. I ran along beside it, crying, and Gran kept telling me to go back.

"I won't go back, Gran! I won't go!" The car picked up speed, little by little. I fell behind. Gran still talked to me through the window, but I couldn't hear what she was saying. Then she rolled up the window and drove away. I ran as fast as I could, but the red taillights got smaller and smaller until they turned into the road and disappeared. I ran clear to the mailbox at the end of the lane, but I didn't see them again. I flopped down by the mailbox and leaned against the post and puked between my knees. I thought I was going to die. I wanted to die. I didn't hear Daddy come, and I didn't see the lantern, but suddenly he was there, and I couldn't move. He stooped and wiped the vomit off of my face and clothes with his handkerchief. He set the lantern on the ground and picked me up and settled me against his chest like a little baby and picked up the lantern again.

"Time to go home, Gate," he said. He trudged slowly back up the lane. The circle of light from the lantern swung back and forth over the ground ahead of us. I still couldn't stop crying, and I kept swallowing, trying to get the vomit taste out of my mouth.

"Don't ever believe in happy endings, son," Daddy said. "There just ain't no such thing."

One day toward the end of that summer I walked into the kitchen and found Mother sitting at the table with her head in her hands. She was kind of sniffing. I stood a minute and watched her. She didn't look at me and didn't say anything.

"Mother?"

"Hmmm?"

"What's the matter?"

"Nothing."

"Then why are you crying?" I came closer and laid my hand on her shoulder.

"I'm *not* crying!" She moved her hands away, and her eyes were full of tears, and her face was red and wet. Then she laid her head on the table and cried real hard. I didn't know what to do. I just stood there, kind of patting her, wanting to get away but feeling I shouldn't.

"Mother, *please* tell me what's wrong."

Her shoulder jerked under my hand, and she sniffed and made little groaning noises like I'd never heard her make before. Then she stopped and sighed and sat there still with her head on the table. She finally said something real low, and I didn't understand her.

"What?"

"Your daddy's going to the Army, that's what," she said, looking up at me. "A farmer, with three kids and another one coming . . . You didn't know that, did you? But it's a fact. And they're taking him." She pointed at the door. "The Allisons sit over there with four grown men to work their farm. Not a single one of them has gone. Why? Because they're too dumb!" She was mad, and she was getting loud. She pointed at the kitchen stove. "And Sam and Louis Bowie sit over there on their place! Both young! Both bachelors! Are they going? No, they're not! Why? Because they're rich, that's why! But Will Turnbolt isn't dumb! Will Turnbolt isn't rich! Will Turnbolt has a wife and three kids and another one coming! Will Turnbolt is going to the Army!"

"Does he have to?"

"Yes, he has to." She was quieter now.

"Who says?"

"The government says. Now, go outside. I've got a lot of thinking to do."

Belinda and Rick were making mud pies under the windmill. I started to go over and play with them, but changed my mind and walked around the house and out the front gate. The lane looked all white and trembly in the hot sun. I started walking. The dry dust oozed between my toes, almost like mud, and my feet left footprints so plain that I could look back and see everywhere I'd been.

I was glad Daddy was going to the Army. I pictured him in a soldier suit with lots of medals and ribbons on it. I pictured him sitting in the drugstore, talking to all us boys, telling us what he did to the Germans and Japs. I pictured him with a steel helmet on his head, like the soldier on the war bond picture at school. I pictured him wearing a flat cap with a bill and an eagle on it, like the soldier who came to school

one day and told us what to do if we found a Jap
balloon in our pasture. I pictured him sending me a
German flag like the one Mr. Stoner had hung up
behind the fountain at the drugstore and a Jap sword
like Jaime Smith's daddy had sent him and also a Jap
knife, small enough to take to school. I pictured our
window with a banner with one star in it, and people
looking at the banner when they drove by our house.
I wondered where we could put the banner so that
they could see it. I wondered why Mother didn't want
Daddy to be a soldier and why we were about to get
a baby and what it would be like. I wondered if Daddy
would talk to me. I turned and walked back to where
Belinda and Rick were playing.

"You know what?" I asked them.

They looked at me, four brown eyes in two brown
faces streaked with sweat and mud.

"What?" Belinda asked.

"Daddy's going to the Army."

"Who says?"

"Mother."

Rick was patting a mud ball into a pie. Belinda
picked up a fruit jar and poured some more water
into her bucket.

"You know what else?" I asked.

"What?"

"We're going to get a baby."

"Who says?"

"Mother."

"Rick's our baby!"

"Not any more. He's getting big, dummy! Where's
Daddy?"

"Down at the barn, I guess."

I found him under the tree in Old Blue's pen behind the barn. His saddle was slung across the top rail of the fence, and he was wiping it with a greasy rag. A can of saddle soap was in his hand. He looked around at me as I came in the gate and sat down on the ground under the tree, but he didn't say anything. He went on wiping the saddle slowly, carefully, now and then bending to take a good look at a scratch or scuffed place. The dark brown leather glistened, and the flower-and-leaf design looked like carved wood. The silver buckles and *conchos* and the big metal horn shone like diamonds. It was an expensive saddle, and I remember that Mother was mad when Daddy bought it, a long time ago. Daddy rubbed awhile, then stepped back to look at his work, then rubbed again. Old Blue was drinking at his trough over in the other corner. He sucked the water noisily between his teeth. His blue hide twitched whenever a fly lit on him, and now and then he slapped himself across the haunches with his tail. Daddy whistled one of his fiddle tunes real low, kind of to himself, and Old Blue craned his neck over in our direction and pricked up his ears. When he found out what the noise was, he didn't pay any more attention to us. He just ambled over to the fence and stuck his head over the rail and looked off toward the bluff, like he was expecting company from that direction.

"Daddy?"

"Hmm?"

"You're really going to the Army, aren't you?"

"Uh-huh."

"When you going?"

"Soon."

"How long will you be gone?"

"I don't know. A long time, I guess." He looked out toward the bluff, too.

"You want me to soap your saddle for you while you're gone?"

"No. Harley's going to take it."

"Aw, Daddy! I'd take real good care of it!"

"Yeah, I reckon you would. But you're going to be busy, going to school and all. It's a big saddle for a little boy. Harley'll take care of it."

"Well, I'll feed Old Blue for you, anyway."

"Harley'll have him, too."

"What about Nero? Will Harley have her, too?"

"Yeah, her, too."

I shut up. I was starting to feel real funny inside I hadn't expected all this. I looked at Daddy standing there in his blue overalls and his straw hat, rubbing that soap into his saddle, and somehow I just couldn't picture him in a soldier suit any more.

"Who says you've got to go?"

"Uncle Sam."

"Who's he?"

"The government."

"Does everybody have to do what the government says?"

"Yes."

"What happens if you don't?"

"You go to jail."

Nero slid under the fence and trotted over and sniffed my leg. She plopped down beside me, and I rubbed behind her ears for her. She shut her eyes and moaned.

"Let me keep Nero, Daddy."

He went on rubbing until he finished up the saddle, put the lid on the can, and lifted the saddle off the fence. Then he turned and faced me, holding the saddle by the horn with one hand and the soap can in the other. The shadow of his hat brim hid his eyes. His jaw was brown, and his white teeth were grinning.

"You're about to learn a few things, young man," he said. "Maybe things ain't been too good on this place with your old man around, but you're about to learn that they can be a damn sight worse without him. And another thing. You're about to learn that a man can even get along without his dog, if he has to."

My father wasn't a cruel man, although the rest of us, in my memory, cried a lot. I remember each of these occasions very clearly. Yet I don't remember hating my father, or even fearing him. I remember him, during the time we lived on the farm, as my hero, my god. I remember following him across the newly plowed black fields, stretching my legs, trying to step from one of his footprints to another, and feeling proud somehow that I couldn't do it. I envied him his shotgun and begged him often to let me shoot it. He never did. But one day, when several families had gathered at Harley May's house and the women were inside quilting and the men, lately returned from the hunt, were lounging on the front porch, drinking coffee, I found his gun among several lying on the grass and decided to pick it up. As I tried to lift it, the breech slammed shut on my thumb. I squealed and dropped the gun, and it fired. My father whipped me before he sent me into the house to have my mashed thumb fixed, but while Mother was wrapping it in a rag I heard him on the porch, laughing and bragging about my wanting so much to shoot the gun, and I wasn't sorry I'd tried. And then there was that Christmas party in the schoolhouse at that tiny community—was it really called Addlepate?—not far from our farm. A lot of the kids got big dolls and trucks and drums and I got only a little glass lantern filled with tiny pieces of candy. But my father took it off the tree and gave it to me from his own hand, and I was happy. These scenes flash through my mind quickly and softly, like far-off shooting stars. They don't lie there and burn in vivid detail.

One evening about sundown, Jim Bob Calhoun, Joe George's father, rode up to the front fence on his big bay while we were sitting on the porch waiting for supper.

"Evening, Will," he said.

"Evening, Jim Bob."

"Been fishing lately?"

"No. Been hunting a lot, though."

"Well, Jake Cassidy says the catfish are biting down on the Bosque, and some of us figured we might get a bunch together and go down, wives, kids and all. Sort of a going-away party for you." His saddle creaked as he leaned forward and crossed his arms over the horn. The bay snorted.

"All right," Daddy said. "When?"

"Day after tomorrow. Bring your quilts and enough grub to last a few days. If Jake's right, we might stay awhile."

"Fine."

"Better be ready pretty soon after noon. We'll honk at the foot of the lane."

"Okay. We'll come running."

"See you."

"Stay for supper?"

"Nope. Virgie's probably waiting supper on me right now."

"Okay. See you."

Mother had me lugging stuff out to the car pretty near all morning, it seemed. There were piles of quilts and pillows, the frying pan, the Dutch oven, the sourdough crock, and cardboard boxes full of food wrapped in wax paper and salt and pepper and flour and corn meal and sugar in glass jars. Daddy was at the tractor shed untangling his trot lines and mixing a batch of chicken blood bait. Mother had fried the chicken, and it lay in the bread box in the back seat, smelling good. I barely had time to dig up two tin cans full of worms from the wet places around the windmill and horse trough before I heard the horn honk down on the road. Daddy came out of the shed carrying a gunny sack full of tackle and yelled at me to hurry. He tied the sack on the fender while Mother piled us into the car, then we took off down the lane.

Three cars and a truck awaited us. There was Jim Bob and Virgie and Joe George, Harley and Ellen May, and a carload and a truckload of Allisons, whose names I could never remember because they all looked alike. Most of the Allison grownups were crowded into the car, and the truck that Bill Allison used to haul cotton and hay was brimming full of Allison children. I didn't know any of them very well because they didn't go to school. Mother said they were all idiots. They lived together in the same house down on Clear Creek, and they were dirty and slept with their socks on.

Daddy pulled our car into line behind the truck, and Jim Bob led us all down the road toward Darlington. As we rode through the town, I watched for the little banners with the stars on them. Some had one star, some two, some three. One had four. The banners hung in the front windows of the white frame houses, and there was one star for each man that house had in the service. There were a lot of banners and a lot of stars—blue for living soldiers, and gold for dead ones. Mrs. Compton's star had turned from blue to gold.

As we passed the red brick drugstore, Mother turned her head and gazed at the upstairs windows. Daddy looked straight ahead, and Mother turned back toward him and smiled faintly. "It's nothing, Will," she said, and he reddened under his tan.

Not far beyond town we turned into a narrow road that went by several farms that I'd never seen before. The road was dry, and the dust from the other cars poured in our open windows and threatened to choke us, but it was too hot to close the windows. Rick cried, and Mother pulled him into the front seat and wiped his face with a wet washrag until he quieted. Belinda and I sat on the piles of quilts and talked about what the Bosque River was going to look like. The only running water we had seen was Clear Creek and the little branch that cut across the corner of our south field and ran down to it. But after a while we were too hot to even talk any more, so we just sat and sweated and reamed the dust out of our nostrils with our fingers. The road narrowed, and tree branches scraped the sides of the car. Finally, to keep them away from our faces, we had to roll the windows up partway.

We stopped, and Virgie got out and opened a wire gate and held it until we all passed through. Then we took off across a pasture with no road at all, toward a long grove, and when we got to the trees, we stopped. The Allisons piled out of the truck yelling, and we got out too, feeling groggy and a little wobbly.

"Where's the river?" I asked.

"Through those trees," Daddy said, and started walking toward them. We waded through weeds that reached clear to my waist, scaring up swarms of grass-hoppers that jumped in front of our faces.

"I don't want to go in there," Belinda whined. Daddy grabbed her up with one hand and Rick with the other and carried them, each under an arm, like two sacks of flour. When we were among the trees, we could smell the river and hear the Allison kids already yelling and throwing rocks into it. I broke into a run. Joe George was standing on a huge rock that stuck out into the water.

"Boy! Ain't this something!" he said. "I never seen so much water!"

"I bet there's acres of fish in there," I said.

The river was about as wide as two houses, and it ran between two rocky banks that sloped down from a grove of trees on each side. It ran slowly, and the sun glared off the little ripples, giving it the appear-ance of a wrinkled, peeling old mirror. It was the grandest sight I'd ever seen.

The women were carrying things down from the cars and spreading them around a big grassy place on the bank. One of the older Allison girls was running around, trying to keep up with Belinda and Rick and all the other Allisons, and Daddy and Jim Bob and Harley and the four Allison men were stringing out the trot lines along the bank and starting to bait the hooks.

"If we hurry and get these hooks wet, maybe we can have fish for supper," Jim Bob said.

"Yeah," Daddy said. "You help me, and I'll take the first line across."

The men stripped down to their drawers, and the Allisons picked up two of the lines and started walking along the bank, looking for good places to string them. Jim Bob tied one end of the remaining line to a small tree near the water's edge, and Daddy took the other end and started wading out. Jim Bob squatted on the bank and paid out the line to him, and Harley kept it off the rocks and snags. The hooks danced a crazy little jig above the water as Daddy pulled them farther and farther away from the bank.

"How's the water out there?" Harley yelled.

"Mighty fine," Daddy said. "I think I'll just stay out here all summer."

"Yeah, and if Uncle Sam wants you, he can just dive in and get you." They laughed. Daddy waded in deeper and deeper until he had to hold his head back to keep his chin out of the water.

"Is that as deep as it gets?" Jim Bob asked.

"It better be. I can't swim, you know."

As he neared the other bank, he slowly emerged and

tied his line and waded back. The line was under water now, and we could just see where it went in and came out. The men sat down on the bank and watched the line.

"We're sure going to miss you, Will," Jim Bob said. "I know me and Virgie sure miss our two boys." He sighed. "But I guess there's nothing to do but hope it don't last too much longer." Daddy and Harley nodded silently. Soon, three of the Allisons joined them. Bill Allison grinned.

"I brought back some brew, last time I was in Waco," he said. "It's iced down in the truck. I sent Lon to get it."

"Son," Daddy said, looking at me, "why don't you boys go get your fishing poles and go sit down there on that rock? There ought to be some good ones down there."

We did, but we didn't have any luck. It was nice, though, just sitting there holding the pole, watching the wind bow out the line over the water, wondering if that cork was ever going to bobble, talking to Joe George about how dumb those Allisons were. Bill Allison was the only one who ever said much. The others just followed him around and did whatever he told them to. The Allison kids made plenty of noise, though, and we could hear them and Belinda and Rick yelling at each other among the trees, playing tag or something in the weeds that Belinda didn't want to walk through. Some of those Allisons were bigger than Joe George and me, but they would rather play with Rick than us. The women were circled on the grassy spot, sewing and talking and laughing.

Every now and then, one of the men flung a beer bottle into the water, and pretty soon it would float by us.

About sundown, the men ran the lines for the first time, rebaited them and came back with enough fish for supper. We ran over to watch them gut and skin the cats and scale the perch.

"Boy, I guess old Jake knew what he was talking about, didn't he?" Daddy said to Jim Bob.

"Yeah, if this keeps up, we might not ever go home."

When Daddy's tin plate was heaping with clean carcasses, I carried it to the grassy place, where Mother and the other women had a couple of fires going and hot grease ready in the frying pans and coffee boiling. It was getting dark, and the air was full of the smell of burning wood and frying fish and potatoes and coffee and sourdough biscuits and the river and the grass and the noises of locusts and frogs and kids and women and grease sizzling and logs popping, and I wished it would never rain or hail so that we could live out there like that forever.

There's just nothing better to eat in the world than fried catfish right out of the pan and sourdough biscuits. We all were so hungry that we just ate and ate and didn't say anything, except every now and then, during a rest, somebody would tell how good he felt. But nobody bothered to answer.

After supper, the men gathered around the fire and drank more coffee and talked, while the women cleaned things up. Joe George and I played hide-and-seek with Belinda and Rick and some of the Allisons for a while, but when we tired of that and started making noises like wild animals to scare the younger

ones and make them cry, the daddies made us all go
to bed. They let Joe George and me sleep together,
though, so we spread our quilts on the bank and lay
and talked for a long time and listened to the water
lap the bank.

I don't know how long I'd been asleep when I heard
the men hollering. I sat up and saw a woman running
down the bank with a lantern, and some of the other
women trying to shush the little kids and keep them
in bed up by the fires. Then I saw Daddy and Bill
Allison walking up the bank holding Lon Allison by
the arms. All were naked, and Jim Bob and Harley
walked behind them, carrying clothes. They were
naked, too. Bill Allison's wife was walking ahead,
carrying the lantern.

"Where are the other boys?" she asked.

"I left them to finish up the lines," Bill said.

They walked Lon over to the fire, and he sat down
and peered at his belly. Bill squatted on the ground
and looked at it, too.

"Something's happened," I whispered to Joe George.
"Come on."

The men looked funny, standing naked in the fire-
light. All the women except Mrs. Allison kept busy
with the children. Lon looked funniest of all. He was
sunburned almost black from the waist up and was
fish-belly white from the waist down, as if he'd fallen
headlong into a deep mud puddle. He stared at his
belly and then gazed up at Bill through long strings
of wet blond hair. His buck teeth glistened in his dark
face.

"It's all right, Lon," Bill said. "Don't worry about
it none."

When Lon moved his hand away from his belly, I saw two small holes and a little blood oozing from them. Mrs. Allison poured coal oil on them and wiped them with a dirty rag. Harley stepped in front of me. "I think we'd better get him in to Doc Kenney, Bill," he said.

"No, no, he'll be all right," Bill replied. "Lon's been bit worse that that before, ain't you, Lon?" Lon appeared not to hear. He watched his mother wipe the holes, never flinching from the coal oil.

"Did you see it happen?" Jim Bob whispered to Harley, not noticing me behind them.

"Yeah," Harley whispered. "Didn't you?"

"I just heard Lon yell something."

"Yeah, he hollered, 'This is for fucking Laverne,' and threw a snake at Will. Will grabbed it and threw it back."

"Jeee-sus!"

"Now come on, Bill, be reasonable!" Daddy snarled from across the fire. "That might've been a water moccasin, for all you know! This boy could die!"

"It wasn't no water moccasin. And even if it was, Lon ain't going to die, and we don't need no doc. None of us Allisons has ever needed no doc, and we ain't going to start now. We've always took care of our own, and that's what we're going to do now."

"But Bill! He *can* die!" Daddy cried.

"Listen, you son of a bitch! You keep talking like that and you won't never call Bill Allison a friend again!" The other two Allisons had arrived with their strings of fish, and they and Bill gathered around Lon and Mrs. Allison as if they expected Daddy to charge them.

"Will's just trying to help you, Bill," Jim Bob said. "Doc Kenney can get that boy well a lot faster than you can."

"You're all a pack of mother-fucking sons of bitches!" Bill was almost foaming with rage. "Lon's my boy, and I'll do with him what I goddamn well please! Now get your asses away from here and leave us alone!"

Daddy took his clothes from Harley, and the three men dressed.

"Gale," Bill said, "go get the white lightning out of the truck. Lon could use a drink." One of the other Allisons trotted off naked through the trees.

"Shit!" Daddy said. Then he noticed Joe George and me. "You boys get back to bed right now," he said, "or I'm going to whip you both within an inch of your lives."

It was about daylight when Mrs. Allison screamed. We were up and running to where the Allisons already were crowding around. Mrs. Allison was lying on top of Lon, screaming. Lon lay naked, not moving. Bill yanked Mrs. Allison off. "Lon's dead! Lon's dead!" she screamed. I glimpsed Lon's belly. It was swollen, the fang marks looking like small dark eyes in a small purple head. Mother and Daddy had come by now, too, and Mother grabbed me. Her hand was trembling.

"Get out of here, Gate!" she said. "Both of you. Go over by the fire and stay with the young ones." She tried to bring the Allison children away, too, but Bill stopped her.

"You leave us Allisons be, Lacy," he said. "This is our business and nobody else's."

He allowed Daddy to stay, though, and we all sat and watched Bill and Daddy and Mrs. Allison fumble with Lon, slapping him, pumping his arms, listening at his chest. Then Daddy and Bill wrapped him in a quilt and carried him through the trees and laid him in the back of the truck. Then they came back and gathered up all the Allisons' gear and loaded it, and the other Allisons piled into their car and the truck and drove off slowly across the pasture.

Daddy walked slowly to the fire, and Mother handed him a cup of coffee. He took a long pull and then stood staring into the graying coals.

"He really was dead, wasn't he?" Jim Bob asked.

"Yep."

"Anything we can do for them?"

"Nope. Bill says the Allisons take care of their own." He threw the rest of his coffee into the fire. "Shit. Well, we might as well pack up, too. I don't think we want to fish any more."

"What about your trot lines?" Jim Bob asked.

"Just leave them. I guess I won't be needing them for a while."

The sun was already hot, and the dust was still bad, and we all found that we were covered with chiggers. It was a long ride home.

The next day, Mother thought it would be proper for us to go see the Allisons and help with Lon's burial. Daddy didn't like the idea. "Bill killed him," he said, "and by God, Bill can bury him." But he finally agreed to go, and Mother began bathing and combing us. Since I could dress myself, I was first into the washtub, which I liked. I hated to bathe after the others, when the water was no longer warm and lapped the thick film of lye soap and dirt onto my skin.

Mother had set out my white shirt and the new pants she had bought at the rummage sale for me. They were the first I had with belt loops, and Daddy had cut down one of his old belts to my size, and I felt big, putting it on. When I was dressed, I sat in the rocker on the front porch to wait for the others and listen to Mother talking to Belinda about her pinafore and Daddy telling Rick to settle down and stop splashing the water on the floor. But I tired of waiting and walked around behind the house and climbed to the top of the cellar and pretended that I was a cowboy hiding out from the Indians. The round earth mound of the cellar was a good place to do that, because I could play like it was a big mountain and the weeds on it were trees, and I could see the Indians riding around the foot of the mountain wondering where I was.

But I tired of that, too, and got to looking at the sheet-iron door that sloped down the side of the cellar to the ground. Finally I slid down it. I didn't go down nearly as fast as I did on the slide at school, but it was fun, and I did it again. Then I started a contest with myself, seeing how fast I could run up to the top of the cellar, slide down the door, and run up again.

Belinda came to the corner of the house and stood watching me. I slid down the door again. When I turned to run back to the top, she hollered.

"Gatewood Lafayette! What happened to your pants?"

The whole seat was ripped. Belinda turned and disappeared, and I knew she had gone to tell on me. I waited for Daddy to appear at the corner with his belt in his hand, but he didn't come. I couldn't decide whether to stay and wait for him or go give myself up.

Then I heard the car start, and I ran to the corner just in time to see it start down the lane. Belinda and Rick waved at me through the back window. I just stood at the gate and watched the car disappear. I was confused. For a minute, I thought they'd just forgotten me and would come back. But I really knew that wasn't true. If it were, Belinda and Rick wouldn't have waved.

Finally I went into the house and put my overalls on again. Then I ran to the barn, climbed the ladder to the loft and over the stacked bales of alfalfa, and dropped the pants into the dark space between the hay and the wall.

The loft was shady, except for the wide beam of white light that poured through the open door where Daddy dropped hay into the milk pen. And it was sweltering. I lay on my back on the hay and watched the sunlight gleam through the nail holes in the roof and listened to the chickens caw-cawing sullenly and Old Blue stomping and snorting. I thought maybe I'd just stay there until Mother and Daddy got home and just let them wonder what had happened to me. I'd just lie there and listen to them calling my name while they searched the farm, and I wouldn't answer. And after a long while, I'd just die in the heat, from hunger maybe, and they would carry my body to the house and lay me down on my bed. They would cry and say, "Oh, if only we hadn't run off and left him!" It would be too late. I'd be dead forever.

But the heat really was terrible, and the hay raised an itch on my sweaty back. I climbed down and went to see Old Blue. He stuck his head over the fence, and I rubbed his nose. His mane was tangled, so I got the curry comb out of his shed and combed it out for him. Then he wearied of me and wandered over to the other side of his pen, so I returned to the house.

I had never been left at home alone before, and I just couldn't think of anything to do. I searched the yard for Nero, but couldn't find her. I wandered to the corner where the soft dirt was and played with the red truck I got for Christmas one time that Rick liked so much. But that was no fun without him and Belinda to play with and argue with, and thinking of them made me feel even worse. I lay on my bed and looked at the pictures in my books, but the house was too quiet, and I thought of death again. I considered going down to the branch and falling and hitting my head on a rock and drowning and letting them find me there and bring me back to the house all wet and dead. I pictured the Allisons coming over to help with the burial and all those kids playing hide-and-seek in the redbud trees while Daddy and Bill Allison dug my grave. "Pipe down!" Daddy yelled at them. "I don't want no laughing while I'm burying my own true son!" Then I reconsidered. Maybe the Darlington cemetery would be better. I'd have one of those pretty tombstones with a little glass window and a picture of the deceased behind it.

HERE LIES

GATEWOOD LAFAYETTE TURNBOLT

(little window and picture)

STRICKEN

AT THE AGE OF ONLY SIX

1944

"Oh, Will!" Mother cried. "Why did we have to run off and leave him? I just bought those pants at the rummage sale!" And Daddy stood there with Rick in his arms, patting him on the back. And Belinda looked up at Daddy and asked, "Can I sleep on the sleeping porch now?"

I went back to the yard, picked up a rock and threw it up onto the roof. It bounced high, hit the shingles, bounced twice more, then dropped to the ground. I threw another one, and it did the same. I threw another one, and another one. I threw a flat one that didn't bounce. It remained on the roof. Then I threw others, trying to knock it off. Then one slipped just as I let it fly, and it shattered the living room window.

The crash and tinkle of all that glass was the scariest sound I've ever heard. I was too frightened to move, or even think. I gazed at that hole where glass used to be but now wasn't, and I envied Lon Allison.

Then I remembered a little square orange can on a shelf in the tractor shed, and I remembered that I asked Daddy once what was in the can, and he said it was glue that would glue anything. I got the can and sat down on the living room floor and gathered the slivers in front of me and tried to figure out how they should fit together. I couldn't make them fit. I seemed not to have enough glass to fill that hole. So I dashed outside again, down the path to the trash pile by the toilet. I raked the pile with my feet, looking for every piece of broken glass, whimpering. I took off my shirt and gathered into it pieces of bottles and vinegar jugs and Mentholatum jars and pie plates and lugged them to the house and laid them on the floor with the broken window. Then I got a knife from the kitchen and pried the lid off the orange can. It wasn't glue at all. It was powder. Some kind of white powder.

The car doors slammed. I pulled the shade over the window and frantically picked up the glass fragments and put them back in my shirt. Suddenly Mother and Belinda and Rick were standing there. And Daddy. They just watched me as I knelt, still picking up glass and putting it in my shirt, and whimpering.

"What happened here, son?" Daddy asked softly.

"I . . . The window broke."

"How?"

"I didn't mean to! You all went off and left me and I didn't have anything to do and didn't have anybody to play with and I was just fooling around and I was throwing some rocks up on the roof and watching them come down and this rock slipped out of my hand and hit the window and . . . "

I talked faster and faster. I was crying and trying to catch my breath and felt dizzy.

Daddy smiled. "That's enough, son. It's all right." He lifted me into his arms. "I've got to bring the cows up. Come along with me. Your ma'll clean this up."

On the porch he pulled out his handkerchief and wiped my eyes. Then he held it over my nose and told me to blow. "Feel better?" I nodded. "Well, let's go take a look at the damage."

He looked up at the window a long time, then looked down at me. "Pretty big hole, ain't it?" he said. I nodded. "But just one pane," he said. "It ain't so bad. I see there's a rock still on the roof." I nodded. "But it ain't doing any harm. I used to throw rocks up there myself when I was a kid. Never broke a window, though." He laughed, and I smiled back at him. "Come on."

We started toward the pasture gate. "Is Lon buried now?" I asked.

"Yeah. Right in his own backyard. Where's your new pants?"

"Behind the hay in the loft."

He laughed. "They must have been pretty bad."

"Tore out the whole seat."

He halted. "Wait a minute," he said. "I want to get something at the barn. Come on."

He closed the feed-room door behind us, and it was very dark. "Bend over that sack there," he said.

"No, Daddy! Please don't! I didn't mean to!"

"Now, hush and bend over there. This might have to last you a long time, and it might as well be one you'll remember."

He shoved me against the sack. I'd never been whipped with the quirt before, and it stung like nothing I've ever felt. I squirmed all over the sack, my feet kicking. I heard myself screaming and Daddy saying, "Hush, now."

He stopped and hung the quirt by the door and waited. "Now, dry your eyes and get on back to the house. We'll have no more crying today."

Despite my stinging ass and legs, I felt calm and clean inside, like a fruit jar that's just been scalded and is standing empty, waiting to be filled with something. Belinda and Rick were in the corner where the soft dirt was, playing with my red truck. I sat down with them, and they stopped playing and looked at me, and I looked at them. Then Rick extended a closed hand and said, "Here." I stuck out my hand, and he put into it a limp piece of something stringy and as long as my little finger. It was damp and brown and dirty.

"What is it?" I asked.

"Shoestring potato," Belinda said. "Mrs. Allison gave us some. Rick saved it for you."

I looked at the potato and then at Rick and then at the potato again. It looked like a worm. Rick watched me solemnly from under his dark curls.

"It's to eat," he said.

I put the thing in my mouth and chewed it up. I never tasted anything so good.

Uncle Toy and Uncle Oscar drove up in their big green car while we were still at the breakfast table. Daddy heard them first and went to meet them. "I'll be damned!" he called out the front door. "What brings you slickers out to the country so bright and early?"

"We got your card yesterday," Uncle Toy said. "We figured if we were going to have a chance to say good-bye, we'd better hightail it. Left Waco at five o'clock this morning. Hello, Will."

"Howdy, Toy. Howdy, Oscar."

"Howdy, Will."

"Well, come on in. You had anything to eat yet? We're at it now."

"Haven't, as a matter of fact. We'd be obliged," Uncle Oscar said.

We all jumped up when they came in, and Uncle Oscar picked up Rick and then Belinda and lifted them high over his head. "Lordy, you kids have grown!" he said. "You all are probably too old to be interested in a red sucker now, I reckon . . ." He reached into the side pocket of his brown-and-white-striped seersucker suit coat and brought out three red suckers, wrapped in cellophane, and examined them quizzically. "What am I going to do with these things?" he asked. "Take them back to Waco, I guess, and give them to some kids that are little." We watched him silently. "Hate to do that, though," he muttered.

"You can give them to us, Uncle Oscar," I said. "We're not that big."

"Oh? Well, all right, if you say so." He handed them over.

"Don't take the paper off until you finish your breakfast, you hear?" Mother said.

We laid them by our plates, and Uncle Oscar and Uncle Toy sat down and loaded their plates with biscuits and gravy and fried salt pork.

"I'll fry you some eggs," Mother said, moving to rise.

"No, no, this is plenty," Uncle Toy said. "There's nothing like country cooking to make a man wish he'd never left the farm."

Mother and Daddy looked at each other and smiled slightly. Uncle Toy was short and pink and fat and bald, except for a row of yellow curls that stretched from ear to ear around the back of his head. His suit was blue, like a preachers', even to the little flag pin on the lapel. His shirt and shoes were glistening white, his tie the same red as the stripes on the flag. He ran a funeral home, and as I watched his pudgy hands break more biscuits for gravy, I wondered if he washed them after handling his dead people.

Uncle Oscar was older, and balding too, but he

looked more like Daddy. His narrow shoulders hunched forward while he ate, the rumpled seersucker sagged away from the collar of his white shirt. He wore no tie. His shirt pocket bulged with pencils, fountain pens and bits of paper, yellow, pink and white. The movements of his long arms swung the coat open sometimes, revealing more pencils and papers in his inside breast pocket. He owned a feed store. His skin was brown, like Daddy's, but wrinkled, and his eyes were larger and looked very sad, even when he smiled at us.

Business wasn't too good, they said. The war had made it impossible to get good help, they said. Daddy sipped his coffee and peered at them through the gray-blue smoke of his cigarette. He said nothing, and they didn't look at him or at any of us while they ate. Finally, Daddy interrupted Uncle Toy.

"You all didn't come down here to tell me goodbye, did you?"

"Well, not *just* that, Will." Uncle Oscar glanced quickly at Daddy, then gazed again into his gravy. "We've got some business to discuss."

"What business?"

"How's the cotton coming, Will?" Uncle Toy asked.

"Fine."

"How's the oats?"

"Fine."

"The hay?"

"Fine."

Daddy's voice was more tense each time he said it. His cigarette butt sizzled as he pressed it into a little puddle of coffee in his saucer, then he pulled his tobacco sack from his overalls and began rolling another, his eyes squinting and aimed through his gold-rimmed glasses at Uncle Toy while he licked the paper.

"Well, who's going to take care of the crops after you go in?" Uncle Toy's pink tongue licked white gravy from his pink lips.

"Jim Bob Calhoun ... Harley May ... the Bowies ..."

"The neighbors, in other words?"

"That's right." Daddy's eyes flickered.

Uncle Toy shook his head slowly. "That won't do," he said. "Neighbors have their own problems. You can't depend on them when you need them."

"*We* can."

"It could mean the end of your crops, Will."

"You mean *our* crops, don't you, Toy?"

"All right, our crops, but ..."

"What Toy's trying to tell you is that we think we ought to have somebody on the farm full-time while you're gone." Uncle Oscar glanced at Mother. "A *man*, that is."

"Where you figuring to put up a hired hand on this place? And who would pay him? You?"

"We weren't figuring on a hired hand, Will. A share-cropper, maybe."

Daddy reddened. Mother paled. "You kids better take your suckers and go out and play," she said.

It must have been about an hour before my uncles left the house, Uncle Oscar looking at the ground and Uncle Toy bowing and walking backward as if conducting the bereaved into the viewing room to inspect his work on their loved one. They shooed us off the fenders of their car and drove away, and I was nearly grown before I really understood the meaning of that morning's conversation.

Gatewood Lafayette Turnbolt, my grandfather, had worn out two wives on that farm; each of them had borne two children. The first, whose name I still do not know, bore Toy and Oscar. The second, Louisa Adamson Turnbolt, bore my father and Mary Louise, who died when she was eight and lies buried under the redbud trees near the junction of our lane with the Darlington road. My grandfather was a frugal man, and saved enough to educate two of his sons—Oscar at a business school in Waco, Toy at an embalming school in Fort Worth. They never again put hand to plow or hoe. My grandfather and my father worked the farm, and when my grandfather fell ill and left all the work to my father, he promised he would make a will leaving his farm to his youngest survivor.

But when my grandfather died that afternoon on his cot in the living room, his face turned toward the window and the redbud trees a quarter-mile beyond, there was no will, and Oscar and Toy returned to bury their father and claim their inheritance. Although they owned two-thirds of the farm, they told my father he could keep it as his home and work it and keep half of all he produced.

In other words, my father was a sharecropper. His brothers were gentlemen farmers who visited their land during quail and dove season and brought their dead birds into our house to be cooked by my mother and eaten at our table. They weren't loved and loving uncles come to share the beauty of our land and the taste of our game. They were our masters, shooting *their* birds on *their* land. And when my father could no longer husband their property, another share-cropper had to be found to take his place.

The farm of which my father owned one-third was a hundred twenty acres of dry, dark country. Generally, there were sixty acres of cotton, twenty acres of oats or barley, a small patch of alfalfa, and the rest was pasture. One-third of that is forty acres. There was a large, old but tight barn with several pens around it, a windmill and water tank, a corn crib so old it leaned. It was infested with rats, which meant that it also was infested with copperheads, which often lay glistening across the path that wound from the house, by the corn crib, to the toilet, an ancient structure which sagged amidst a juniper brake fifty yards from the house. There was a tractor shed and workshop outside the front yard fence, and another small shed (the function of which I can't remember) behind the house, near Mother's garden.

The house was of unpainted pine, aged silver-gray. A long, drooping porch was its entrance. There was only one bedroom, a large living room, a kitchen with running cold water and a kerosene range, a long room once used for storage which served as a dining room when the crowd was too large for the kitchen. Rick and I slept there in winter. In summer we slept on the screened-in sleeping porch off the kitchen. Belinda slept always in the bedroom with my parents. The kerosene range and a wood stove in the living room warmed us in winter. Three kerosene lamps were our light. I cleaned their chimneys, trimmed their wicks and filled them with oil every Saturday.

It was said that Turnbolts had lived on the place

since the time of the Civil War. I don't know whether that is true. It was said that many Turnbolts were buried in the vicinity of the redbud trees. But my father's sister, his father, his mother and the wife who was before her possess the only markers there.

It was my birthday. I got up early and peered through the screen to see what kind of day I was going to have. The air was so clear and the sun so bright that you would have thought somebody had come along during the night and given the whole world a fresh coat of paint. The chickens looked like big glistening snowballs wobbling slowly around the barnyard, and Nero, chasing her own shadow or some animal or bird that I couldn't see, bounded near the back doorstep. The windmill whirred in the warm breeze, and the suckle rod, whispering its gentle "thunk-thunk," lifted the water and splashed it into the tank. It looked like a good day to be seven on.

Rick's dark hair was barely visible at the top of his sheet. He slept soundly. The quiet told me I was the first up, but then the front screen slammed, and soon I heard Daddy's fiddle. He was playing something slow and sad, something not right for a morning like that. I sneaked out the door and moved slowly toward the front of the house and sat down on the ground near the corner and listened. Daddy finished the sad tune. Then he started a happy one, "Cotton-Eyed Joe," I think, but stopped in the middle and didn't play anything for a minute. Then he played another sad one.

The dog found me and started romping around and climbing on me and licking me, trying to get me to play with her. I tried to shoo her away without making any noise, but Daddy noticed the commotion and came around.

"I wasn't doing anything," I said.

"I know."

He was all dressed up in his blue suit and white shirt and red-and-blue tie, and he had on some new brown shoes and a gray felt hat with a brim that came over his forehead. I'd never seen him so dressed up.

"You going somewhere today?"

"Yes."

He plunked the fiddle strings with his thumb, as if trying to make sure it was in tune. I began to understand what day it was.

"To the Army?"

"Yes. To the Army."

"Will?" Mother's voice drifted through the front door.

"Yeah?"

"Come on in. Breakfast is ready, and the kids are getting up. You seen Gate?"

"Yeah. He's here."

"Tell him to come on in. We don't have much time."

Daddy grinned and reached out and messed up my hair. "Go get some clothes on," he said. I'd been standing there in my drawers.

They were all around the table, pouring Post Toasties into their bowls, when I got there. Rick and Belinda were still yawning and rubbing at their eyes.

"I wanted to fix you a good breakfast this morning," Mother said, "but we got up so late, and you don't have much time."

"This is okay," Daddy said.

We ate quietly and fast. When he had finished his

cereal, Daddy took out his watch and looked at it. "I ought to have time for another cup of coffee before Jim Bob gets here," he said.

"I could have taken you in," Mother said. "The mail truck won't leave Darlington for two hours. You'll just have to sit around and wait." She poured his coffee.

"Well, Jim Bob was going in anyway, and there's no use wasting gas." He rolled a cigarette and lit it and slouched back in his chair and looked at us all, one by one. "You kids behave yourselves while I'm gone," he said. "Don't give your ma a hard time."

"We won't, Daddy," Belinda said solemnly. Rick shook his head.

Daddy grinned and blew a cloud of blue smoke toward the ceiling. "Make sure you remember that," he said. He finished his coffee and put out his cigarette in the bottom of the cup. "Well, I'd better hit the road." He got up. Mother looked kind of funny, kind of small and scared and sad, and Daddy put his arm around her and said, "Don't worry, Lacy. I'll get a leave pretty soon." He kissed her on the cheek and then walked around the table and kissed us all on the cheek, then walked into the living room. We all followed.

Our old brown leather suitcase was standing by the front door. Daddy picked it up and started to leave. Then he turned and put the suitcase down and kissed all us kids on the cheek again and gave Mother a long kiss right on the mouth. It made me feel uncomfortable, like I was seeing something I wasn't supposed to.

"Goodbye, Lacy."

"Goodbye, Will. Take good care of yourself."

"I will. You, too. Goodbye, kids." He picked up the

suitcase again and opened the screen door, and then just stood there holding it open and looking at us. "Come along to the road with me, Gate," he said.

When we passed by the tractor shed, he stopped and took a long look at the old Farmall sitting there, the big toothlike lugs on its iron wheels glowing in the shadow. Then he turned and looked toward the house. Mother and the kids were out by the fence, and I could tell that Mother was crying. They all waved, and Daddy waved back, then we started down the lane again. "I ain't going to look back no more," he said. We walked along quietly and slowly, and Daddy looked at everything as we went by, as if it was all new to him and he was trying to find out what it was all about. He looked real good, dressed up like that.

"Are you going to stay gone a long time?" I asked.

"Maybe. Maybe not. Nobody knows for sure."

"Where are you going? I mean, where is the Army?"

"North of here a-ways."

"Will you send me a Jap knife, when you get a chance?"

He laughed. "Yeah, *if* I get a chance. It'll be a while, though, so don't go running to the mailbox every day."

The lane stretched clean before us. The sunflowers couldn't have been yellower and the sky couldn't have been bluer, and Daddy looked at it all. "Pretty day," he said. "Don't remember a prettier one. I wish it was raining."

"Why?"

"I don't know. I guess it would be a little easier to leave if it was raining. Maybe not, though."

We sat down by the mailbox, but we weren't there long before we saw Jim Bob's old blue pickup coming down the road. We stood up, and Jim Bob stopped.

"Ready, Will?"

"Ready as I'll ever be, I guess."

Daddy threw his suitcase into the back and opened the door. He had one foot on the running board and was about to climb in when he turned and looked at me.

"Today's your birthday, ain't it?"

"Yeah."

He stuck his hand into his pocket and pulled out his old bone-handled pocket knife and grabbed my hand and put the knife in it. He kind of grinned and messed up my hair again. "It ain't a Jap knife, son," he said, "but happy birthday." He climbed in, and Jim Bob slammed the pickup into gear and took off. I watched until they disappeared over the hill.

When Harley and Ellen came to get Nero and Old Blue was when I really knew we were moving. Harley stepped out of the pickup and hollered to the house.

"We're here to get them, Lacy," he said, and Mother just waved at him through the screen, and he walked to the barn and saddled Old Blue and rode him back to the house. Then Ellen opened the pickup door and tried to whistle Nero in with her. Nero just stood there wagging her tail, looking at Ellen, then looking at Harley up on Daddy's horse. We were all standing at the living room window, staring out, and I asked Mother if I could go say goodbye to Nero.

"No," she said, "because then she wouldn't go, and things are hard enough without that. Just keep still."

Harley and Ellen kept trying to talk Nero into jumping in with Ellen, but she wouldn't, so finally Harley climbed down and picked her up and threw her into the pickup and slammed the door. Nero yelped and jumped against the window, but Ellen threw the pickup into gear and took off down the lane. Harley mounted and followed her at a lope.

The next day, Bill Allison came with his truck and his two boys and hauled our stuff to the little white frame house on the hill by the schoolhouse in Darlington, where Gran lived. A greasy sharecropper named Shipp and his ugly wife and about fifteen kids moved into our farm like a band of Comanches. Mother and I walked around the place with Shipp, and Mother showed him where things were and told him what to do. "They're white trash," she said as we drove back to town, "but they're all we could get."

Then school started and I was in the second grade. My new room was next to my old one, but I didn't like it as much, and I didn't like my new teacher. Her name was Mrs. Potter, and her hair was always messed up and she smelled like cooking cabbage and had a mustache. Sometimes during recess I would go back to my old room and talk to Mrs. Brim, and she would try to get me to like Mrs. Potter, but I never did.

All I had to do in the morning was walk out the back door and across a little pasture and crawl through a barbed-wire fence and I was on the school ground. Sometimes I'd go over there on Saturdays, too, and play around on the slide and swings, but it wasn't much fun.

Gran took me to church every Sunday. Sometimes she would take Belinda, too, but she always took me. It was time I learned about Jesus and all he did for me, she said.

"Hurry up, Gate. Your Sunday clothes are on the chair in the living room. Drink your milk."

"Can I have some coffee milk, Mother?"

"Drink it down some first. There's not room for coffee in that glass."

I closed my eyes and drank it down about an inch. It stuck to the inside of my mouth. Mother filled up the glass with coffee, and I reached for the sugar bowl.

"*One* spoonful," Mother said. "Unless you've got a pocketful of sugar stamps on you. Where's Rick?"

"On the pot," Belinda said. "He's always on the pot."

"Ricky!"

"Huh?"

"Get up and eat."

"Okay. Through." He staggered in, pulling up his drawers, and sat next to Belinda.

"Oh, Rick!" Mother said. "Why didn't you wait until I wiped you? Damn it. Come on, Gate. I've got to get you ready. Bring your coffee with you."

I put on my Sunday shirt and sat down to button it. "Your fingernails are filthy," Mother said. She took her toothpick out of her mouth and started digging with it.

"Ouch!"

"Hush. You want to go to Sunday School looking like Filthy McNasty?" She spit on her hand, wet my cowlick and combed my hair. Then I stepped into my blue Sunday pants and Mother hooked up my elastic suspenders and the elastic band of my tie. "There," she said finally. "Now you look like a gentleman."

The downtown street was deserted, except for a few cars headed toward the same place Gran and I were going. The drugstore, Thompson's Texaco, the Helpy-Selfy Laundry, Pearly White's blacksmith shop all were locked with big padlocks. The Johnson grass in the cracks of the concrete floor of the old burned-out bank building had turned brown, and shivered slightly in the cool breeze. We played marbles around chalk-drawn circles there in the spring, but I knew all those circles had been washed away by now.

Gran parked in the big gravel square in front of the big white frame Baptist Church. The square was always full of cars on Sunday, because all three of Darlington's churches were there—the Baptist on the west, the Methodist on the north, the smaller Camp-bellite church on the south. On the east was the tabernacle where all three took turns holding revivals in the summer.

"Have you got collection money?"

I shook my head, and Gran dug in her purse and handed me a penny. "Now, give it to Mrs. Arnett when she asks for it," she said, "and don't lose it."

We were late, and the Primary Class was almost through singing when I got there.

I've got that Bap-tist boos-ter spi-zer-inc-tum
Down in my heart,
Down in my heart,
Down in my heart!
I've got that Bap-tist boos-ter spi-zer-inc-tum
Down in my heart,
Down in my heart to stay!

It was the song we always sang during the revival, when the Primary Class became the Baptist Booster Band and we banged sticks together, clanged cymbals, and hit triangles with ten-penny nails.

Mrs. Arnett's rump was bothering her again. She had a little inner tube that she brought to Sunday

School to sit on when her rump was bothering her, and she was sitting on it today. She told us the story about Moses and the bullrushes. The girls always loved that one, but the boys liked David and Goliath and the one about the man who killed all those guys with the jawbone of a jackass. After the story, Mary Jean Haskell passed the basket around for us to put our pennies in. She got to do this because her daddy was the preacher. Then we colored until the bell rang. I colored a picture of Noah letting a bird go while all the animals watched. I colored the bird blue.

"Oh, Gate, you never color right," Mary Jane said. "Doves are white."

"I haven't got a white Crayola. Blue's better, anyway."

"And Noah's face isn't black. It's white, too. He wasn't a nigger."

"I told you once, I haven't got white!"

"You can't even stay inside the lines!"

"Leave me alone!" I was getting pretty riled, and Mrs. Arnett got off of her inner tube to come over and shush me, but the bell rang, and she had to go stand by the door and hand us a picture when we went out. Mine showed Jesus talking to a man up in a tree.

"It's got a story on the back, Gatewood," Mrs. Arnett said. "Get your grandmother to read it to you."

"I'll read it my own self."

"My, you must be a smart boy." Mrs. Arnett smiled and patted my head, then shoved me out of the door.

I found Gran in the auditorium and sat down by her. Brother Haskell came in, and we had some songs and some prayers, then they took up another collection. This time, Gran gave me a nickel to drop into the plate. Then Mr. and Mrs. Tyler came in and sat down by me. They always came in after the collection. Mr. Tyler was big and round and wore a wide belt with curlicues on it and a big shiny buckle. The belt squeaked like a saddle when he breathed, and I watched the buckle move up and down while Brother Haskell talked. Gran nudged me. She pointed at Brother Haskell. He was red in the face, and he was yelling about a collie dog he used to have that got caught in a house fire, and how that dog yelped and hollered, and how his hair and flesh smelled while he was burning up, and how that was just what hell was going to be like for those who were going. And I started thinking about Nero, and how I'd feel if she got caught in a fire like that and I couldn't get her out.

Finally, he slowed down enough to tell us we were going to sing a song, and he came down and stood in front of the pulpit, and everybody sang.

> *"Al-most per-suad-ed," now to be-lieve;*
> *"Al-most per-suad-ed," Christ to re-ceive;*
> *Seems now some soul to say,*
> *"Go, Spir-it, go Thy way,*
> *Some more con-ven-ient day*
> *On Thee I'll call."*

A couple of high school girls came down the aisle crying. Brother Haskell whispered in their ears, shook their hands, and waved them toward the front pew. Then he started shouting again, shaking his fist, his oily black curls dancing over his eyes.

"How do you know the sun's going to come up tomorrow?" he yelled above the music. "How do you know you won't depart this world tonight while you're asleep and go to your grave with your sins still strangling your soul? Do you want to burn like my collie dog forever and ever?"

Gran was crying. Tears were dripping off her chin. She took off her glasses and wiped her eyes with her handkerchief.

"Al-most per-suad-ed," harvest is past!
"Al-most per-suad-ed," doom comes at last!
"Al-most" can-not a-vail;
"Al-most" is but to fail!
Sad, sad, that bit-ter wail,
"Al-most," but lost.

That was the end of the song, but Brother Haskell wasn't through yet.

"All right, brothers and sisters," he said. "All right! I know the Spirit is working in some of your hearts today. There's still time! There's still a chance to get through the gates of heaven before they slam shut! I want every head bowed! Every eye closed! If your husband, your son, your mother is lost, pray for God to send the light! If you're a sinking sinner, throw your life into the Everlasting Arms right now!"

We bowed our heads, and I gnawed on a corner of my Jesus picture.

"Almighty God, who canst read our evil hearts like an open book, we know the day is coming soon when we will stand before thy judgment bar . . ."

Brother Haskell prayed a long time, but nobody else was saved, so he finally told everybody to come down and shake hands with the two high school girls. People started moving into the aisles, and Gran put her wet handkerchief into her purse.

"How did you like the service today, Gate?"

"Fine."

"Well, you were a good boy. Now, go wait for me in the car while I go down and extend these girls the right hand of Christian fellowship."

As we rode toward home, Gran waved at people getting out of their cars in front of their houses and hummed a song.

"Gran," I said.

"Hmmm?"

"Can I stop going to church again when Daddy gets home?"

She looked at me kind of funny. "Don't you want to go to heaven?" she asked.

"Yeah, I guess. But do you have to go to church to do that?"

"Yessirreebobtail," she said.

"I guess Daddy won't be going then, huh?"

"I don't want to stand in judgment of anybody, but I'll be mighty surprised if I see him there."

Everybody was supposed to take a nap on Sunday afternoon at Gran's house, and everybody did except me. I never could sleep in the daytime, so I'd usually just lie on my bed and look at my books until everybody else went to sleep, then I'd go outside.

As I stepped out the door, Alice Childers was walking across the road from her house, which was next door to the Haskells'.

"Come over and play," she said.

"I can't. I'm taking a nap."

"You ain't."

"Well, I'm supposed to be. I'm not supposed to leave the yard anyway."

"A little while won't hurt."

"What do you want to do?"

"I don't know. Let's go watch Mary Jean's toilet."

The Haskells had a new house, which Brother Haskell built himself when he wasn't preaching. It had the only flush toilet in Darlington. It was white, and when you pushed a handle, water ran through it and gurgled, and all the shit disappeared.

"You think Brother Haskell will let us watch it?" I asked.

"I don't know. Maybe he's taking a nap, too."

Mary Jean and Alice were both third-graders. I never played with Mary Jean because I didn't like her. She thought that because she was older than I was, she could boss me around all the time. But Alice never let on that she was older than me, and I liked her a lot. I would go to Mary Jean's when Alice was with me.

We knocked at the front door. No answer. We knocked again. No answer.

"Let's go around back," Alice said.

No answer there, either. The car shed door was open, and the car was gone.

"Maybe they're eating with somebody," I said. "Let's see what's in the car shed."

It was shady and warm inside. There was a workbench with a bunch of tools in one corner and a big pile of straw in the other. I could smell the spot of oil on the ground. An old tire was hanging on the wall.

"Let's shut the door," Alice said.

"What for?"

"Just to see what it's like."

"It'll be dark."

"Scared?"

"No."

"Then shut the door."

I swung the two big doors shut. There was a window over the workbench. I could see the sunlight through some nail holes in the shingles, too. Alice sat down in the straw. She looked like a fat teddy bear with bangs.

"See, I knew it wouldn't be dark," she said.

"Well, what'll we do now?"

"Let's fuck."

"What's that?"

"I'll show you."

She yanked up her dress and pulled down her drawers. "Take your thing out and put it in there." She pointed.

"Why?"

"That's how you do it."

"I don't want to."

"Oh, come on. It won't hurt you."

"How do *you* know?"

"Because I saw my big brother do it to Billie Ann Caldwell in our well house, and it didn't hurt him none."

"Yeah, but he's in the Air Corps!"

"Well, Billie Ann ain't in the Air Corps, and it didn't hurt her, either."

"Well, it still seems like a dumb thing to do."

"Oh yeah? Well, your own daddy does it."

"How do you know?"

"All daddies do it. He does it to your mother. My big brother says he does it to Laverne Thomas, too."

"How does *he* know that?"

"Laverne told him. My big brother does it to Laverne, too."

"Well, I'm still not going to. I'm going to open the door."

"Wait a minute!"

She yanked her drawers up just as the doors swung open. We walked outside.

"You won't tell, will you?" she said.

"No."

"Promise?"

"Yes."

"Cross your heart and hope to die?"

"Cross my heart and hope to die."

"Let's go swing. I'll let you be first."

"Okay."

We ran across the vacant lot between the Haskells' and the Childers', and I picked up the swing board and set into its notches the rope swing hanging from a limb of Alice's chinaberry tree. I sat down, and Alice gave me a shove, and I rose into the air. The wind whistled in my ears. Alice shoved again and again, and I rose higher and higher. I rose until I was almost level with the limb the rope was tied to. I pretended I was a pilot chasing a Jap plane. Alice was panting.

"Alice! Don't swing him so high! You want to break his neck?" Mrs. Childers was at the upstairs window. She was fat and ugly and hung down in front. She didn't have a dress on, and as I sailed back and forth across the window I could see her big old tits about to fall out of her slip. Alice stepped back and let me coast down, and Mrs. Childers disappeared.

"My turn now," Alice said. "Pump me." She sat down on the board, and I straddled her, standing up. There was barely room for my feet between her fat legs and the ropes. I grasped the ropes, bent my knees, pushed my body down. We moved. I kept pumping, and we went higher and higher, almost as high as I went with Alice pushing me.

"We better coast now," Alice said. "Mama'll yell at us again." Slowly we coasted to a stop. "Push me," she said.

"No. It's my turn. You push me."

"No. I pushed you longer than you pumped me."

"No, you didn't."

"Yes, I did."

"No, you didn't!"

"Yes, I did!"

"Didn't, didn't, didn't!"

"Did, did, did!"

"Didn't, didn't, didn't!"

Alice jumped out of the swing and socked me on the ear. I let out a yell and grabbed the swing board and ran for Gran's house. Alice took off after me. I was getting scared, and yelling, and tears were coming into my eyes, and I could barely see. I could hear Alice panting behind me. She grabbed for me and caught my suspenders. The clamps popped off the front of my pants. She pulled on the suspenders. By now, we were across the street. Gran was standing on the porch. Alice let go and ran for home. The suspenders popped me hard in the back. I yelled again, grabbed my pants, and ran up the sidewalk and up the steps. I looked back. Alice wasn't in sight. Gran hugged me to her and wiped my nose with her skirt.

"Come on inside, Gate," she said. "I'll read you the funnies. We'll see if Dick Tracy's caught The Brow yet."

I dropped the swing board behind the honeysuckle bush.

I've often wondered why, of all the experiences I

must have had during my father's absence, that Sunday has remained so vivid in my mind. Years later, when the storms of puberty wracked my mind and loins, Technicolor dreams of that fat little girl in the straw, panties at her feet, skirt turned inside out over her breastless torso, haunted me. Never mind that Gatewood Lafayette Turnbolt at seven couldn't have satisfied Alice Childers even had he been willing. I could at least have paid closer attention, been curious, explored with eye and finger and gotten a preview of the joys and tribulations that lay ahead. Even now that my virginity is long since gone, Alice Childers still intrigues me. Who finally accepted her invitation? How long after she extended it to me? Did she remain fat, or did she grow into beauty? Is she now a housewife? A waitress? A professor? A whore? Whatever she is, she is lost to me. Just one vivid memory of a hazy but crucial time.

But there are flashes of others. Virgil Stoner, the druggist's son, came home with a chestload of medals and only one leg. He jerked down the Nazi flag that he had sent his father and that Mr. Stoner had displayed so proudly behind the soda fountain. Virgil sat at one of the little round marble ice cream tables for two or three days, his crutch lying beside him on the floor, saying hello to his friends and neighbors from before the war. Then he went home and shot himself with a German pistol. I was an anti-aircraft gunner during recess at school. I sat astride a long piece of pipe like a stick horse and blasted away at the sky. Golden Patricia Cabell was always near me. I jerked my head back and crumpled to the ground as some invisible German or Jap pilot (the entire Axis was our foe on the school ground) got in his licks. Patricia lifted me gently, I hung my arm around her neck, and she and I struggled together back to our fort. She was a good nurse. The wound wasn't fatal. Joe George Calhoun was waylaid by a bunch of "big boys" in the school privy. They removed his overalls and shorts and tossed them up on the roof. "Eat it up, wear it out, make it do, or do without" crossed my grandmother's lips at least once a day. The radio spoke daily of the Allies and the Axis, Roosevelt and Churchill, the White House.

And my father came home once, after his basic training, I suppose. He wasn't in uniform, but he brought me and Belinda (now five) and Rick (almost three) each an overseas cap and patted us all on the head and sat and talked to us for a while as if we were somebody else's children. Then Mother came out of her room with a little suitcase, and she and my father got into the car and drove away. Gran came out of the kitchen, where she had stayed during the time my father had been in the house. "Come on, kids, I'll read you a story," she said. My father and Mother were gone all the next day. I heard them come in during the night, but when I got up the next morning, my father was gone.

"Virgie and Joe George are going to stay with you a few days, so you all behave yourselves and do what she says."

"Where are you going?" Belinda asked.

"To the Comanche hospital to get our new baby," Mother replied, "and Gran's got to take me."

"Couldn't you take yourself?"

"Well, yes, but Gran's going to help me pick out the baby we want."

"Why can't *we* help pick it out?"

"Because they won't let kids come into the hospital, that's why," Mother said, laughing.

"We could stay outside by the alligator pond, and you and Gran could bring some out and let us pick one," I said.

"That's a good idea!" Mother said, laughing again. "But I don't think the doctor would let us do it."

"Why?"

"Well, does Mr. Stoner let you take candy out of the drugstore before you pay for it?

"No."

"Well, that's how the hospital is, too. You have to pick while you're inside."

The day was dark gray. The wind wheezed in the treetops. I carried Mother's suitcase to the car. Virgie and Joe George were driving up.

"You didn't pick a very good day to go, Mother," I said.

"No, but it'll have to do."

"Don't worry about a thing, Lacy," Virgie said. "Everything's going to be all right, I promise."

"Hi," Joe George said. "Brrr!" He hugged himself.

"Hi," I said.

"I believe you, Virgie," Mother said. "We just have to trust in the Lord."

Gran was shooing Belinda and Rick off the porch back into the house. When she had put her suitcase into the car, she bent and kissed me and hugged me. The big fur collar of her coat smelled cold and dusty. Then Mother kissed me, too.

"Remember, you're the man of the family," she said. "Help Virgie every way you can."

"I will."

Virgie put an arm around Joe George's shoulders and the other around mine and hustled us into the house. As soon as we slammed the door, she pulled a brown paper sack from under her coat, held it high and said, "Well, who wants a cookie?" Rick started crying. She picked him up and carried him to the kitchen, sat him in his high chair, put the cookies on a plate and poured milk for all of us.

"You all help yourselves," she said, "but stay in the kitchen until you're through. We don't want to mess up Miss Gloria's sitting room, do we?"

She handed Rick a cookie, and he started gnawing on it and pretty soon forgot to cry. We sat around the table and ate.

"Which would you rather have, a brother or a sister?" Virgie asked. We all looked at each other. Belinda shrugged.

"I don't guess it makes much difference," I said. "Maybe a sister, since we've already got two boys."

"What's a hospital?" Belinda asked.

"It's where they take people that are real sick," Joe George replied.

"Mother's not sick!" Belinda yelled. Then she looked at me, worry in her big brown eyes. "Is she, Gate?"

"Of course not!" Virgie said. "Your mother's fine! The hospital's a healthy place, and they keep the little babies there until they're big enough to take home, and then the mothers and daddies come and get them."

"Our daddy isn't here," Rick said.

"I know, honey," Virgie said. "But he'll be home someday, and won't he be surprised when he sees what your mother's got!"

"He already knows about it," I said. "He knew about it before he went to the Army."

"Oh, of *course* he did! He probably helped your mother fill out the order."

"Why don't we fill out an order, Mama?" Joe George asked. "Gate's already got Belinda and Rick, and now he's getting a new one. I'm tired of being the littlest one in our family."

"Finish your milk," Virgie said. "Let's clean up these crumbs, or Miss Gloria will be awful mad when she comes back."

Sleet was slapping at the windows now, and the wind was higher than ever. Joe George and I sat by the window and watched the lights of the cars moving slowly up and down the road and listened to the wheezing of the two big elms in the front yard. The lights were on in some of the houses, and Virgie turned ours on, too. She sat on the floor by the big coal oil stove and played with the little ones, but they didn't seem to want to play very much, and I was getting tired of looking out the window and talking to Joe George. It got pretty quiet, and Rick started crying again, and Belinda looked like she was about to, and I wanted to.

"Anybody want any supper?" Virgie asked. Nobody answered. "Too full of cookies, huh? Okay, then, time for bed."

She said Joe George and Rick and I could sleep on a pallet on the floor, just for the fun of it, and I helped her get the quilts down and undressed Rick while she attended to Belinda. Belinda climbed into Gran's bed with Virgie.

The pallet was thin, and it took us a while to get comfortable, but things finally got still, and Virgie was snoring softly, and Joe George's breath came slow and heavy, and I lay there staring up into the darkness and listening to them and to the wind and sleet. I was thinking I was the only one still awake when Rick slid over to me and whispered in my ear.

"I wish Mother was here," he said.

"I do, too," I said. I put my arm around him.

Virgie fixed us oatmeal with prunes in it for breakfast and dressed the little ones and shooed Joe George and me out the door into the cold. The storm was over, and the sun was out, but the little white sleet pellets still lay on the dead grass and crunched under our feet as we walked across the pasture to school.

All the kids crowded around me when they found out that Mother had gone to get the baby. The girls especially liked babies, and they all wanted to know if they could come see it when Mother brought it home. Even old Mrs. Potter smiled a little and let us talk for a few minutes after the bell rang before she told us to shut up and sit down.

As Joe George and I walked back across the pasture after school, Virgie came out on the back porch and yelled at me. "Hey, Gate!" she said. "You've got a new baby sister!"

"Yippee!"

I ran for the house. Virgie told us all to get in the car and go with her to the grocery store, and we could tell everybody. She drove us all over town, and we stuck our heads out the windows into the cold and yelled the news. The little ones bounced on the back seat and chanted, "We've got a baby si-i-i-ster! We've got a baby si-i-i-ster!" over and over again, and people in cars and on the sidewalk smiled and waved.

"Your grandma called Mrs. Haskell not an hour ago," Virgie said. "She said it weighs eight pounds, and your mother named it Cherry Ann."

"When are they coming home?" I asked.

"Miss Gloria said Saturday, and an ambulance will bring your mama."

"An *ambulance*! With the siren and red lights and everything?"

"Maybe. We'll see."

"Boy howdy!"

We waited for Saturday like Christmas. Belinda and Rick were always asking Virgie, "Is it Saturday yet?" and she would laugh and say, "Not yet. I'll tell you when." But Saturday finally came, and when it came it was cold. Virgie wanted us to stay inside, but we couldn't, at least Belinda and Joe George and I couldn't. We sat at the top of the front porch steps, all capped and coated and gloved, watching our breath steam out before us in the still, clear air. We looked up and down the street and listened for the siren and talked about Mother and Cherry Ann and wondered how much hair our baby sister would have and what color her eyes would be. But the ambulance didn't come, and we would get too cold and have to go inside and stand by the stove. Rick, all cozy in corduroy, watched us puff and blow our hands.

"Saturday yet?" he asked.

I laughed. "Not yet, but pretty soon."

And when we were toasted, we would go back out and sit some more, and then get up and wander around the yard, wanting to do something besides just wait, but not knowing what. Finally, I climbed the mulberry tree in the backyard. The tree wasn't as tall as the house, so I couldn't see anything, but I shaded my eyes with my hand and squinted like I was looking way off down the street.

"See anything?" Belinda asked.

"Yeah, I see the street . . . way, way down the street, clear to the highway . . . and a bunch of cars . . . a big, long black car . . . It's the ambulance! The ambulance is coming! Hurry, Belinda! Run to the front, or you'll be too late!"

Belinda took off around the house. I climbed down, and Joe George and I sat under the tree and giggled until Belinda came back, and then we put on serious faces again.

"It's not there!" Belinda said. "You're telling a story!"

"Doggone!" I said. "I thought sure that was it."

Joe George got up and walked around the other side of the house, and pretty soon he came running and yelling, "It's coming! It's coming from the other way! Hurry, Belinda, or you'll miss it!"

And Belinda took off again. We kept up this game until Belinda got tuckered out and looked like she was about to cry. "No fair, Gate!" she said. "You keep on fooling me!"

Her brown eyes looked so big and hurt that I felt kind of ashamed of myself, so I held her in my lap and played with the curls that were sticking out from under her red knit cap, and pretty soon she grinned at me, and everything was all right again.

Virgie came out and told us to come in and eat, and we missed the ambulance. We were halfway through our soup when Gran opened the door.

"Yoo-hoo!" she hollered. "Anybody home?"

We jumped up and ran outside, and there was the ambulance already pulled up outside the front gate, and two men in white coats rolling out the stretcher with Mother on it. No siren, no lights, no nothing. Virgie held us back on the porch while Gran went out and took a little bundle of blanket from one of the men. She carried it to the house, and we all crowded around, saying, "Let me see! Let me see!"

"No, no," Gran said. "Stay back until they get your mother in."

Mother's hair looked bright red against the sheet of the stretcher. She smiled at us when they carried her up the steps, but she looked tired and pale, and she didn't say anything. We waited until the men came back out with the stretcher, and Gran came to the door and said, "You can come in now, but don't make any noise. The baby's asleep."

We tiptoed, but Gran still said, "Shh!" Mother had been laid in Gran's bed, and the little bundle of blanket was in the crook of her arm. She reached over and folded some of the blanket back and showed us the little red baby.

"Ooooo! Little!" Rick said, reaching toward it.

"No, no! Don't touch," Gran whispered. "You'll wake her up."

"She *does* look like a cherry, doesn't she?" Belinda whispered to me.

Mother stretched her arm toward us, and we went up one by one and hugged her and kissed her.

"My babies!" she whispered. "You're all my babies!"

Later, Virgie handed Mother an envelope. "Here's something that'll make you feel better," she said. "A letter from Will."

Mother tore open the envelope. There was just one sheet of paper inside. She read it quickly and dropped her arm onto the bed and looked at Gran, even tireder than before.

"Will's been hurt," she said.

My father and several others had been crossing a bridge across a rocky ravine, and somebody blew up the bridge with a hand grenade. One soldier was killed, and my father and the others fell to the bottom of the ravine. I never knew where it happened, except that it wasn't overseas. My mother got a letter from him occasionally while he was in the hospital, but she never read them aloud to us as she did before the accident. And she never smiled when she read them to herself. She read them once, then put them into their envelopes and put them away in her cedar chest.

My mother sent my father some money that my grandmother gave her, and he sent us some presents. Rick got a little donkey carved out of cedar, and Belinda got an Indian doll wrapped in a little red blanket. I got a leather case with some crayons and a comb and nail file in it. "Souvenir of Hot Springs, Ark." was printed on all of them. My father sent my mother a little leather coin purse which she said he made in the hospital.

My father had sent my mother two photographs of

himself before the accident. In one, he was in dress uniform and was grinning. In the other, he wore a helmet and was holding a rifle, and his face was smeared with black grease paint. My mother told us it was taken when he was training for night fighting. She had kept those pictures on her chest of drawers and had shown them to people who came to visit us. But a few weeks after the accident, she took them down and locked them in her cedar chest, and only occasionally took them out and looked at them. I never knew why.

I was sitting at the kitchen table, trying to build a windmill with my Tinker Toys, and Mother came in and sat down across from me. She watched me for a while, and then she said, "I don't believe you've got enough Tinker Toys there to finish the job, Gate."

"Well, you can build a windmill with them. There's a picture of one right here on the box."

"Yes, but that's what you can build if you have the *big* box. You've got the little one. See? Here's one that shows a motor operating something. You don't have a motor in yours."

"Well, what *should* I build then?"

"Here's a good one. Try a giraffe."

"Okay." I started taking the windmill apart.

"I'll help you," Mother said. She scooted her chair over by mine, and we sat there together, pulling the sticks and knobs apart.

"Your daddy's coming home," she said quietly.

"He is? When?"

"Pretty soon. Soon as he gets out of the hospital."

"To stay?"

"Yes, to stay." She was peering at me very closely, as she did when trying to find out if I was lying about something.

"Can we go back to the farm then?"

"Maybe. I don't know. I don't know how things are going to be."

"Things will be just like they used to be, won't they? Before Daddy went to the Army?"

Mother sighed. She had been twiddling with a Tinker Toy stick, staring at it. Now she looked at me again. "Things never are just like they used to be, Gate," she said. "I don't know how they'll be, but they won't be just like they used to be."

"Daddy's all right, isn't he?"

"I don't know. He hasn't told me." She sighed again. "Well, that's enough of that," she said. "Let's build this giraffe."

Belinda and Rick and I were waiting at the gate when the mail truck drove up. We'd been waiting a long time, and it was almost dark. The driver got out, pulled Daddy's suitcase out from among the mail bags, and carried it to the porch. "Well, kids," he said as he passed us, "there's your daddy!"

Daddy sat in the truck, looking at us through the windshield. We hung back, kind of bashful, not knowing what to do or say. He didn't wave or smile or anything. We didn't either. It was hot and still, and we were standing there in just our shorts. Sweat was popping out on our foreheads.

"Is that Daddy?" Rick whispered to me.

"Yes," I whispered back.

The driver started back now, and Mother and Gran

were with him. Mother was carrying Cherry Ann. Gran was whispering something to the driver. They were hurrying.

The truck door opened now, and I could see two feet under it, and then two walking sticks. Daddy scooted out slowly and stood beside the truck. The door slammed. He was bent. He stood there, hunched over the sticks, his gray felt hat pushed back from his face, his red-and-blue necktie hanging untied around his neck. Mother ran, Gran ran, we all ran. There was a lot of kissing and hugging and crying, and nobody even saw the mail truck leave.

"Hot, ain't it?" Daddy said. "Ought to be good for the oats."

He lay on his back on the floor and lifted Cherry Ann into the air and made funny noises, as he used to do with Rick. But he never laughed at her gurglings. At night, he played dominoes with Mother and Gran, as he used to. But he never argued, never accused them of cheating. Used to, when he lost, he'd get up and stomp out of the house. Now winning and losing seemed the same to him. He went downtown once, on a Saturday, when all his friends would be there. But he didn't stay long, and when he returned, he had Belinda pull a kitchen chair up to the living room window that faced the little empty pasture between the house and the school grounds. He sat down, and with his two hands lifted his legs, first one and then the other, and placed his feet on the window sill. He sat there all afternoon, smoking, never speaking, staring out. We crossed the room on tiptoes and whispered when we spoke at all.

But on the morning of the livestock show he awakened me with the tip of his walking stick and asked me if I wanted to go.

"Sure."

"Hurry, then. I want to see the cattle before the crowd gets there and the tent gets hot."

He was wearing his Army boots and khaki pants, but with a blue, short-sleeved work shirt with washed-in grease stains on it. I held his two black walking sticks while he lifted his legs into the car and tucked them under the steering wheel, and when I got in on the other side, he looked at me and grinned, for the first time, I think, since he came home. He lifted his hand, folded it into a fist, and struck his thigh.

"They're getting better, by God!" he said. "They ain't as heavy to lift now. Pretty soon, they can lift themselves, by God!"

"Will we go back to the farm then?"

"You bet your bottom dollar."

He was still smiling as he backed the car slowly into the road, eased his foot from brake to clutch and shifted into low. "Fact is," he said, "I been thinking I ought to go out there and take a look around the place. There'll probably be a lot of fixing up to do after that cropper gets his crops in and gets out. Maybe I'll go tomorrow."

"Can I go with you?"

"I reckon."

We parked in front of Dale's Dry Goods, and Daddy motioned for me to bring his sticks around to his door. He lifted his legs over the running board, pulled himself up on the open door, and took the sticks. "Let's go in here a minute," he said.

In the middle of the store, between the yard goods and the shoes, was a table full of straw hats. Daddy headed directly for it, leaned his sticks against the table, picked up a yellow hat just like the one he'd worn before he left for the Army, and put it on. He tugged the brim. "I guess I should have gotten a haircut first," he said. "I might get it too big."

"It looks fine, Will," said Mr. Dale, coming up from behind a pile of shoe boxes. "What size is it?"

"Seven and an eighth."

Mr. Dale shook his head and picked up another hat. "This one's for you," he said. "You always wore a seven, and you probably do now. I doubt if the Army put any weight on your head."

Daddy didn't respond to Mr. Dale's grin. "I reckon you're right," he said. "You got one for the boy, too?"

"Yessir. We just got a shipment of cowboy hats in, chin strings and little sheriff's badges on them. They're still in the stockroom, but I'll get one for you, young man."

"No," I said. "I'll just take one like Daddy's, if you've got it."

Daddy grinned and tousled my hair. "This boy ain't no cowboy, Mr. Dale," he said. "He's a farmer like his daddy."

We left the car at Dale's and headed for the big circus tent that had been raised on the vacant lot behind Pearly White's blacksmith shop. The cool breeze tugged at the flat brims of our new hats and threatened to carry them away, since they weren't yet molded to our heads. Daddy dropped a stick to grab at his. I picked up the stick and tried to hand it to him, but he waved it away.

"It's all right," he said. "You carry it. I better hang onto this here hat."

Walking was hard work for him. His Army boots dragged through the grass. The dew gathered into little drops on the oiled leather. But when he noticed the bellowing of the cows and the crowing of the roosters in their wire cages under the tent, he grinned. "That's real music," he said.

We stepped into the shade, and he stopped and looked a long time down the aisle between the rumps of Jerseys and Guernseys tied up to two long ropes that were stretched like fences down the sides of the tent. The place reeked of cow, and Daddy threw his head back and sniffed like a hound dog does when you hold a piece of meat above his head. Then he took his second stick from me and moved down the aisle to where a big, fresh, soft cow pie was, and he looked at it a second, slowly lifted one foot, stepped right in the middle of it and moved his foot around until about half of his boot was just covered with shit.

"Well, I'm really home now," he said.

"Gollee! Why did you do that?" I asked.

"All the time I was in that hospital, every time I thought about home, the smell of cow shit came into my nose. I promised myself that when I got back, I was going to step in the first cow pie I saw."

He laughed, then stuck his other foot in the wrecked cow pie and moved it around, too.

"I always said you was crazier than a hoot owl, Will, but by God, now I got proof."

Harley May had sneaked up behind us and was standing there with his hands on his hips, his yellow teeth shining in his turkey-head-red face. He pushed his hat back and scratched. "Lordy," he said, "I never seen a man love cow shit so."

"There's worse things," Daddy said as he shook Harley's hand.

"Yeah, I reckon. Like the coffee they're selling here. Want to go get a cup, and see if I ain't right?"

"You buying?"

"Yep."

"Hell, yes, then. It ain't every day Harley May flings away a nickel."

We walked toward the other end of the tent, Daddy and Harley stopping now and then to admire a heifer, then went on outside to the coffee man's counter. He had two big enamel coffeepots sitting on a wood fire behind the counter and was pouring the contents of a third pot into a big crock on the counter. When he saw us, he reached into the crock with a water dipper and filled two tin cups on the counter.

"This batch any better than the last one, Jeremy?" Harley asked. He reached into his long, black change purse and put a dime on the counter.

" 'Fraid not, Mr. May," Jeremy said, dropping the dime into the pocket of his brown-splotched apron. "I don't believe the Lord himself could make coffee to suit you. Ain't you going to buy something for the young'un?"

Harley looked down at me. "What you got for young'uns?"

"Sody pop. Red and Dr. Pepper."

"You don't feel like having one of them, do you, Gate?" Harley asked.

"I'll have me a Dr. Pepper."

"I was afraid of that." Harley frowned and undid

the clasp on his change purse again and fished out another nickel. Then he said, "While we're dealing in all this big money, Will, I might as well make you another offer."

"I ain't selling," Daddy said.

"A hundred and fifty for horse and saddle, Will. That's my final offer."

"I ain't selling."

"Let's move over there," Harley said, waving his cup toward a bench under a tree. "There's no use in letting old big-ears Jeremy know our business."

"I ain't heard a word, Mr. May, but I would appreciate you moving on and making room for a more satisfactory customer."

Daddy eased himself down onto the bench and propped his sticks beside him. Harley squatted in front of him, rolled two cigarettes, lit them both and handed one to Daddy.

"You know damned well that horse ain't worth that much," Harley said.

"He is to me," Daddy replied.

"You had a better offer?"

"Nope."

"What you going to do with him, then?"

Daddy squinted. "What the hell you think?" he said evenly. "I'm going to ride him."

"Oh." Harley glanced at me. "You going back to the farm, then?"

"Yep," Daddy said. "Back to the farm."

"When?"

"Soon as Shipp can get his crops in and get out. By Christmas for sure."

"You told him yet?"

"I'm going out tomorrow."

"You talked to Oscar and Toy?"

"What have they got to do with it?"

Harley shrugged and peered at the ground, puffing slowly on his cigarette. Daddy smoked quietly, too, his eyes focused on the long lock of Indian-black hair that spilled from under Harley's greasy straw hat. It was quiet for a very long time, it seemed.

"How's Nero?" I asked.

Harley jerked his head up. "She's fine," he said. "You ought to come out and see her sometime." He grunted and pulled himself off his haunches. "Well," he said, "I'd better go find Ellen. I promised her some foolishness money today, and I'd rather go find her than have her out on the street hollering for me."

"Okay, Harley," Daddy said. "See you."

Harley started away, then Daddy called him and raised his empty coffee cup. "This ain't worse than cow shit. This *is* cow shit," he said. "Thanks, anyway."

Harley grinned and waved, then headed toward Pearly White's.

We were sitting on the bottom row of the bleachers watching the judging of the dainty little Jerseys when the woman sat down by Daddy. She was wearing a tight, short-sleeved red blouse and a black skirt and high heels. Even hose. Her lips were very red, her eyes were very blue, and her blond hair was short and very curly.

"Hello, Will," she said.

"Hello."

"You mind if I sit here?"

"No."

She leaned around him and smiled at me. "I see you have a friend with you," she said.

"Yeah, that's Gatewood," he said. "Gatewood, this is Mrs. Thomas."

"How do you do, Gatewood?"

"Pleased to meet you, ma'am."

She smiled at Daddy. "He's got good manners," she said.

"If he ain't, it ain't because he ain't been taught. How's the telephone business?"

"Oh, the same people are still calling the same people. Still saying the same things to them, too, I guess."

Daddy concentrated on the judge in the ring, who was eying the pin bones and hocks of the little Jerseys and feeling their bags and tits. Mrs. Thomas watched Daddy, a kind of pleading in her blue eyes, and she would glance at me and smile when she saw me looking at her, but the smile would fade when she looked at Daddy again.

"You haven't been to see me, Will," she said finally, very softly.

"No."

"Why?"

The new yellow hat turned slowly toward her.

"Why do you think I'm sitting on the bottom row of these bleachers, with people and dogs walking by and blocking my view?"

"There are places without stairs, Will, if that's what you mean. We could go . . ."

"It ain't just that. The climbing, I mean." He slapped his thigh. "These things are practically dead, Laverne. How . . . You know what that would be like?"

"Listen, Will." She was talking in a fast, earnest

whisper now. "When Jake got killed, I thought I was going to die, too. You knew that, and you saved me. Now . . ."

"Me and Lon Allison and how many others?"

She blushed. "Now, don't get nasty, Will," she said. "I admit there for a while I was a little . . . available. But that was before you, Will, and you know it."

Daddy was looking out at the cows again. He said nothing. She watched him, seeking his eyes.

"There never was Lon, if it makes any difference to you," she said.

"It don't." He looked at her and must have smiled, because she smiled at him.

"Bastard," she said.

"Wench," he said.

She smiled bigger then. "You'll be at the top of the bleachers before you know it," she said.

"Yeah."

"Will you come see me?"

"Yeah."

"When?"

"Not long."

She smiled and touched his arm, then stood and started to walk past us. Then she stopped in front of me and smiled again and opened her shiny black purse and dug in it.

"Gatewood," she said, "would you let me buy you a cold drink before you leave today?"

"Sure, ma'am."

She handed me a nickel. "Make it a red one, will you?"

"Sure, ma'am. Thank you."

"You've got a nice friend there, Will," she said. "He's very polite."

We watched her walk away, then Daddy looked at me. "She's a nice lady," I said.

Daddy bent near my ear. "Now, listen, Gate," he said. "I'd appreciate it if you wouldn't tell anybody about the little talk we just had. Don't tell anybody we saw Mrs. Thomas, and don't tell anybody about her giving you a nickel, or anything else. Let's just let it be our secret, okay?"

"Okay."

"Cross your heart, now?"

"Cross my heart."

"Our secret forever, right?"

"Okay."

"Well, then. Let's go get that red cold drink."

Mother looked worried when she came out to the front porch with us. Rick was with her, and he looked worried, too, as he often did. He was a solemn kid, his almost-black eyes always looking questions at people. He clung to Mother's skirt this morning, kind of hiding behind it, actually, peering around at us. He'd never seen anyone walk like Daddy walked now, I guess, and he didn't know what to think of it. It took Daddy quite a while to get down the four front steps, and we all sort of held our breath while he struggled. But he was getting pretty good at such things, and no longer cussed every time he moved a foot, as he had when he came home. His legs really were getting better, I guess.

"You be careful, Will," Mother said. "No telling what that Shipp might do. I wouldn't trust him for a minute."

Daddy, now at the bottom of the steps, peered up

from under his new hat. "No need to worry, Lacy," he said. "I'm just going out there for some information, that's all."

"I know. But I know you're not going to like him, too. You watch your temper, you hear? Remember, no matter how bad things look, we can always fix them up after we get out there."

"My temper?" Daddy pretended to be surprised. "Why, Lacy! You're talking about a helpless cripple! What's all this carrying on about temper? I'm harmless!"

Mother's frown unfolded into a smile. "You'll never be harmless, Will Turnbolt," she said. "You just mind what I say and be careful, you hear? And drive carefully, too. It looks like it might shower before you get back."

Daddy bowed slightly over his sticks. "Yes, ma'am," he said. "Whatever you say, ma'am."

Mother smiled all the time I helped Daddy into the car and carried his sticks around and got in myself. And still smiling, she waved as Daddy backed the car into the street. Rick still peered silently from behind her skirt.

"Aw, women are funny, Gate," he said. "They worry and worry and worry, but a man can kid them out of anything."

"How come?"

"Oh, I don't know. Maybe they don't really want to believe anything's wrong, and they're just looking for somebody to tell them everything's all right."

"*Is* anything wrong?"

He grinned. "Very little, I guess, all things considered. For a while there, things looked pretty dim, but they're looking better all the time. I guess when a man's been in the hospital as long as I was, it just takes a while for him to start feeling like a man again. I been thinking a lot about some of the other folks in that hospital, and I know things could have been a hell of a lot worse for me. I'll be on my tractor plowing again before some of those guys figure out who the hell they are. Some of them never will figure it out, I reckon."

"Could I go hunting with you sometime?" I asked.

"You might. By the time I get ready to go again, you'll be big enough, I reckon. Me and you and Harley'll just sit by the fire and listen to the dogs all night."

We were passing the churches now, and all three congregations were singing. Gran was there, I knew, and I tried to find her car, but we passed too fast.

"The Christians sure are making things hot for the devil today, ain't they?" Daddy said.

"Did you have to go to Sunday School when you were little?" I asked.

"Nope. My daddy didn't believe in it. My mother neither. It's no place for a man."

"Gran says you're not going to heaven."

He laughed. "She's probably right."

"What would you do if Jesus came back?"

"Offer him a smoke, I guess."

"Doesn't it worry you? Going to hell, I mean?"

"No. The company's liable to be better there. The Baptists will be up there looking sour and singing and I'll be down there chasing foxes with Harley, like I always have."

"Brother Haskell says people burn in hell, in lakes of fire, forever and ever."

"Well, that's just what he *hopes* it's like, since he ain't going there. He sees people like me and Harley sleeping late on Sunday, and going hunting, and carrying on, and he says, 'Well, those sinners seem to be having a lot of fun. More fun than me. That ain't right, since I'm good and they're bad. Why do you reckon the Lord lets them get away with it?' So he sits and figures, and then it dawns on him. 'I know!' he says. 'The Lord's going to make me happy when I die, and he's going to make Will Turnbolt as miserable as hell when he dies.' And that makes him feel better. Trouble is, he can't think of any way to be happy, even after he dies. He just talks about walking on golden streets and resting in the bosom of the Lord. If I had my druthers, I'd pick somebody else's bosom."

"How do you know all that if you never went to Sunday School?"

"I went to a revival once, right after your ma and I married. Brother Haskell wasn't preaching, but they all preach alike. Let's stop here a minute."

We were on the old plank bridge that crosses Clear Creek. Daddy killed the engine and looked at me. "What do you hear?" he asked.

"Nothing."

"Listen harder."

"I hear the creek."

"Yeah. You hear the water splashing over the rocks under this bridge. When I was your age, this bridge wasn't here. We had to ford the creek in the wagon. But the noise of the creek was the same. Water falling over rocks. The rocks down there are round and smooth. All the corners have been worn off of them by the water. They were already that way when I was your age. They were already that way when the first

Turnbolt was born. Maybe even when the first man was born. And when the last man dies, they'll still be there, just like they are now. Maybe just a tiny bit smaller. Now, I reckon that tells us something about God. He made some things that last forever, but man ain't one of them. And as for that bosom-of-the-Lord business, I can't think of any reason why the Lord would want any one of us anywhere near his bosom or any other part of him. I just can't see the Lord getting all excited about the Haskells of this world. Understand?"

"I guess so."

He grinned. "You really don't, do you?"

"I don't think so."

"Well, you will someday. You just try to remember and see if your old daddy ain't right."

He started the car again and drove across the rickety old planks, on down the road to home that I hadn't traveled in almost a year. It was a rainy summer, and the Johnson grass and sunflowers stood higher than the fence posts between the road and the fields. Daddy drove slowly, trying to keep the tires in the deep ruts that no amount of county gravel could keep from being rolled into that soft land in a rainy season. The country looked familiar to me, and yet somehow new. When we had moved to town, it had been later in the summer—almost the end, in fact—and things were more brown and gold than green. It had been a drier summer, too, probably.

When Daddy turned into our lane, he stopped again and pointed through the windshield. "Well, there it is," he said. "By God!"

Our name was still on the mailbox, but somebody

had scratched an X through it with a nail, and the X had rusted. "Turnbolt," Daddy said. The wind was whispering in the redbud trees and parted the Johnson grass sometimes, revealing the white stone beyond the fence that I knew stood over the grave of my grandfather. The house and tractor shed at the end of the lane were very dark under the clouds, almost the color of the earth itself. I could see four light forms moving in the yard. Some of Shipp's children, playing, probably, in the soft dirt in the corner where Belinda and Rick and I used to play. It started sprinkling, and Daddy turned on the windshield wipers and moved the car toward the kids, his eyes glistening behind the gold-rimmed glasses.

He saw Shipp's rump sticking out from under the hood of the tractor in the shed and stopped. The three girls and the little boy stopped their playing and watched me through the fence as I got out and brought Daddy's sticks around to his door and waited while he got out. The front gate was off of its hinges, I noticed. Somebody had tried to tie it back up with baling wire, but it still slumped open. Shingles had blown off of the porch roof, leaving a hole as big as a bushel basket that nobody had taken time to fix. Shipp had come out from under the tractor hood and was walking toward us, wiping his hands on a rag. Grease streaked his face and matted his shaggy blond hair. He didn't recognize me, I knew. And I guess he'd never seen Daddy, because he nodded and looked at him kind of funny when he came around the car and saw him hunched over his sticks.

"Howdy do," he said.

"Something wrong with the tractor?" Daddy asked.

Shipp nodded. "Carburetor, I think. Gas squirts out all over the engine when I crank."

"Hmpf," Daddy said, kind of smiling. "I'm Will Turnbolt. I own this place."

Shipp nodded curtly. "I'm Jack Shipp. I work it." He looked down at his hands, rubbing very hard at the edges of his fingernails with the rag.

Daddy watched him, kind of smirking. Then he asked, "How are things?"

Shipp still rubbed. He nodded again. "Okay, I guess," he said. He looked up. "Want to come in out of the rain?"

It was falling harder. The children left the corner and scrambled up the porch steps. They stood in a row there, watching us. Water dripped from my hat brim now, and Daddy's, and I could hear it drumming on the tin roof of the tractor shed.

"I didn't come out here for no visit," Daddy said. "I just want the answers to a couple of questions. When do you think you can get your crops in?"

Shipp shrugged. Water was trickling down his cheekbones now, and spattering at our feet. I was getting pretty wet and wished Daddy would hurry so we could get back in the car. "It's too early to tell," Shipp said. "You ought to know that."

Daddy smiled and nodded. "Well, I just wanted to tell you to get them in as soon as you can, because we're moving back. You better start looking for another place to go."

Shipp squinted. "Says who?"

"Says I. I'm giving you notice, man. Be out of here, lock, stock and barrel, by Christmas."

Shipp grinned and stuck the rag in the hip pocket

of his overalls. "And who's going to work this place then? You?" His eyes started at Daddy's eyes and traveled down his body, down the rain-darkened khakis to the shit-and-mud-covered boots, planted now in a shallow puddle.

Daddy sneered back. His grip tightened on the crooks of his sticks. "That's right," he said slowly. "Me."

Shipp giggled. "Somebody's been telling you stories, Mr. Turnbolt. Jack Shipp works this place. And them that put him here tells him he can stay as long as he wants to. They been telling him he might get a visit from some cripple in town. They been telling him to tell the cripple to come and talk to them if he had to talk to anybody. 'Don't let him make you no trouble,' they said. 'Just tell him to see us, and we'll put him straight.' I don't know if you're that cripple, Mr. Turnbolt, but it appears like you could stand some straightening out. I recommend those two gentlemen to you."

Shipp jumped back as Daddy's stick swung out and up. He held it high over his head like a saber. He bared his teeth and groped forward with the other stick, slowly following it with one foot and then the other. Shipp took another step back, his grin fading. "Shit, man," he said, "What you up to?"

"I'm going to kill me a fucking sharecropper," Daddy said softly.

Shipp stepped back again, then stopped and grinned when he saw how slowly Daddy had to move. "Is that the way you did it in the war, soldier boy?" he said. "No wonder it's taking us so long to get it over with."

Daddy swung his stick hard. He missed, and the other stick slipped. His body swerved, shuddered and fell, slowly, it seemed, like a tree, belly down, in the mud. I yelled and ran to him, but he pushed me away. His mouth, now muddy, flashed a strange grin, and tears filled his eyes. He planted his hands in the mud, lifted his top half, and dragged his legs slowly toward one of the column posts of the tractor shed.

Shipp glanced nervously at me, and then at Daddy. "Shit, man, I'll help you," he said. "I didn't mean nothing."

"You keep away from me, white trash!" Daddy hissed. He wrapped his arms around the post and pulled himself slowly to his knees. "Bring me the sticks, Gate," he said. He was breathing real hard. I held out the sticks, and he took one, and, bracing himself between it and the post, finally pulled himself to his feet. He stood puffing, looking at Shipp, then at me. Then he started through the mud toward the car. "Pick up my hat, Gate," he said.

When he'd lifted his legs over the running board and closed the door, he started the engine and turned on the windshield wipers. As I trotted around the front of the car, he was staring through the rain at the kids on the porch, and they were staring back at him. If they'd moved a muscle since the rain started, I couldn't tell it.

Shipp came around to Daddy's window. "I could have kicked you in the head while you were down," he said.

Daddy nodded. "Someday you're going to wish you'd did it," he said.

He didn't speak all the way back to town. He just

hunched over the steering wheel, trying to keep the tires in the ruts and out of the soft mud. We'd left the windows down while we were at the farm, and the seat stank and felt clammy against my wet clothes and warm skin. I wiped the fog from my window sometimes, trying to see out, but there was nothing worth seeing, so I quit and laid my head back.

He turned at Pearly White's and parked in front of the little white telephone office behind the drugstore.

"You wait here," he said. "I'm going in here and call your Uncle Oscar."

Daddy had broken down his shotgun on the kitchen table and was cleaning and oiling the parts the next day when Uncle Oscar and Uncle Toy knocked. I was sitting with him, watching. He'd said I could if I wouldn't ask him any questions. Daddy paused and cocked his head when he heard the knock and Gran going to answer the door. When he heard Uncle Toy saying hello, he started wiping the piece he held in his hand again.

Gran came to the kitchen door and said, "I think you'd better come out, Gate, so the men can talk privately."

"He's all right, Gloria," Daddy said. "Let him be."

Gran pursed her lips and raised her eyebrows, then disappeared.

Uncle Toy was mad from the start. "What do you mean calling us down here like this, Will? What's the emergency?"

Daddy didn't look up from his work. "Afternoon, Toy," he said. "Pull up a chair. You, too, Oscar."

Uncle Oscar's sad eyes shifted nervously around the

room. He raised his hand in a little wave to me and formed "Hi" with his lips but didn't say it. He saw the two chairs over by the cabinet, moved them over by the table, motioned Uncle Toy toward one and sat down in the other with a sigh. His face was gray and haggard.

Uncle Toy was flushed and splotchy, and the yellow curls that ringed his head seemed to stand out like little springs. They jiggled when he moved. He had on his blue funeral suit with the flag on the lapel, but his collar was unbuttoned, and his red tie hung loose at the throat. He folded his arms on the table and glared across at Daddy.

"All right, Will," he said. "Let's get to it right now. You told Oscar there's an emergency. What is it?"

Daddy swung the shotgun barrel up toward the window over the sink and peered through it like a telescope. "It's amazing how dirty a gun can get just sitting in the closet for a year," he said. "Rust and moth do corrupt, don't they, Oscar?"

Uncle Oscar smiled faintly. "Yeah, Will, I reckon they do," he said. "Leastways, that's what the Good Book says."

"Did Toy tell you that?" Daddy asked. "He knows all about the Good Book, don't you, Toy? Couldn't hardly run your business without it, could you, Toy?"

"Never mind *my* business!" Uncle Toy yelled. "I want to know why you called us down here!"

"*My* business," Daddy said, laying the gun barrel on the table.

"*Your* business?"

"Stop playing like you're a goddamned idiot, Toy. I need to talk to you about the farm."

Uncle Oscar's hand started shaking. He took an Eversharp pencil out of his shirt pocket and twisted the eraser, running the lead up and down. Uncle Toy calmed down a little.

"All right," he said. "The farm. What about it?"

"Me and Gate took a ride out there yesterday."

"What for?"

"To see how things looked. And to tell Shipp to get off."

"Why?"

"Things ain't too good out there, you know. That son of a bitch don't even know how to crank a tractor right."

"Why do you want him off, Will?" Uncle Toy was quieter now.

Daddy picked up the trigger mechanism and squirted some solvent into it with an eyedropper. "I want to move back," he said quietly.

"You . . ." A wave of Uncle Oscar's hand cut Uncle Toy off.

Daddy looked up at Uncle Toy. "I want to be back on that farm by Christmas," he said. He glanced at me with a very slight smile. "Shipp was very polite. He told me I should talk to you about it."

Uncle Toy's pink hands flew into the air. "Impossible!" he yelled. He jumped up and walked to the other end of the table and leaned over Daddy, shaking his finger. "You talk about me being a goddamned idiot! What do you think of talk like that? You don't know how hard it is to get help these days! We're damned lucky Shipp is out there! No, Will, you ain't going back!"

Uncle Oscar waved his pencil back and forth, like

he was trying to erase Uncle Toy's words. "Now, take it easy, Toy," he said. "Will just wants to talk, that's all."

"No, it *ain't* all!" Daddy yelled. "I want to go back!"

Daddy's sticks were leaning against the table beside him. Uncle Toy grabbed them up like a bouquet of funeral flowers and shook them in Daddy's face. "What are these?" he asked. "Are they planters? Are they harrows? Are they even shovels? No, by God! They're walking sticks! They're your walking tools, Will! You couldn't get across this room without them!"

"I ain't always going to be this way!" Daddy yelled. He started to try to get up, then didn't. "I'm getting better! I'm not going to be using those things always!"

"By Christmas?" Uncle Toy asked quietly. He smiled sadly, shaking his head.

"I wouldn't have any field work to do before spring," Daddy said. "Gate and Lacy could help me with the animals."

"We got no guarantee that you'll be ready to work even by spring."

"You got my promise."

"You can't make promises for your legs, Will."

"Couldn't you take that much of a risk?"

Uncle Toy shook his head.

"What's a man supposed to do, then? I got a family to support, you know."

"You can work for me," Uncle Toy said.

"Doing what? I couldn't carry your carcasses for you."

Uncle Toy shrugged. "We could think of something. Driving the hearse, maybe. Times being what they are,

I don't think it would hurt none to have a veteran in the organization. Especially if he's . . ."

"A cripple?"

"I wasn't going to say that, Will."

"It don't matter. You were thinking it. Oscar?"

"Huh?"

"What do you think, brother?"

He shrugged. "I ain't got a job for you, Will. Lifting those feed sacks and all . . ."

"That ain't what I'm talking about. Me and you own most of that farm. If you say so, I can go back."

Uncle Oscar twisted the eraser, carefully watching the lead slide out of his Eversharp. "There's nothing I'd rather do, Will. You know that. I'd give anything in the world if I could . . ."

"Get out."

"What?"

"You heard me."

Uncle Oscar slid the lead back into his Eversharp and stuck it in his shirt pocket. The chair scraped the bare wooden floor as he scooted it from the table and stood up.

Uncle Toy smiled, buttoned his collar and pulled his tie knot taut. "Let's go, Oscar," he said. "I got some work to do."

Uncle Oscar paused at the door. "I'm sorry, Will," he said. "You've got your disability pay coming, anyway."

I felt the yank on my arm and woke up. Rick was standing by my bed, stark raving naked, yelling, "Up! Up!" and jerking my arm every time he yelled.

"Cut it out, Rick! What do you think you're doing?"

"Up! Up!"

"Rick, now, stop it! Get out of here!"

He grinned, his brown eyes twinkling behind the row of tiny freckles across his nose. I laughed, and leaned over and grabbed him under the arms and yanked him onto the bed. I straddled him and played like I was socking him again and again in the face.

"Pow! Pow! Take that, and that, and that!"

He started giggling and wiggling around, and I rolled over like he'd knocked me off of him, and he climbed on me and started pounding me on the chest. Then he stopped, breathing hard, and looked down at me like he was wondering what to do next. I tickled him in the ribs, and he fell over on the bed, squealing and wiggling.

"Gate!" Mother called from the kitchen. I smelled coffee and bacon.

"What?"

"Leave that kid alone and get up. Breakfast is nearly ready."

"Okay." Rick was lying on his belly, his white rump gleaming in the sunshine. "Get up and get some clothes on," I said.

"Can't."

"Why not?"

"Got to potty."

"Well, go on."

"Come with me."

"Oh, all right. I'll sure be glad when you learn to wipe yourself."

"Me, too."

I got up and put on my shirt and overalls. Rick grabbed my finger, and we walked to the back porch, where the pot was, and he sat down.

"Gate, come on! Breakfast is ready!" Mother yelled.

"I can't. Rick's on the pot, and I'm helping him."

"Well, tell him to hurry."

Rick was grunting and red in the face. "Aren't you through yet?" I asked.

"No."

"Well, hurry. I can't stand here all day."

I heard a footstep behind me and turned. Daddy was standing in the doorway. He looked like he'd just gotten up. His hair was all messed up, and black whiskers were standing out on his face. He had his pants on, but just the top button was buttoned. The fly was open, and his belt wasn't buckled. He wasn't wearing a shirt, and I could see his ribs sticking out, even under his undershirt. He leaned into his sticks. His eyes looked small and very black behind his glasses, and I felt like they were boring two holes right through me.

"What's the trouble?" he asked. His voice sounded funny, like he needed to clear his throat.

"Nothing. Rick's on the pot, and I'm going to wipe him when he gets up."

"Breakfast is ready. Can't you hear?"

I didn't say anything.

"Can't you hear?"

"Yes." Rick was still grunting behind me.

"Well, why don't you come, then?"

"Rick's not through."

Daddy moved past me and stood looking down at Rick. Rick glanced up, then lowered his head again and looked at Daddy's knees. He was still grunting. His face was still red.

"Get off the pot, Rick," Daddy said.

"I'm not through," Rick said.

"Get up anyway."

"No."

"What did you say?"

"No."

Daddy's right hand dropped a stick, and his belt came out of the belt loops like a black snake. It whistled and smacked down hard across Rick's small shoulders. Rick screamed, and he and the pot turned like they were about to topple over, but they didn't. Rick stuck to the pot like he was glued to it. Daddy hit him again, and this time Rick fell forward, and the pot flew into the air and spilled. Daddy hit again and again. I was crying now, and I turned to run into the house, but Mother was coming through the door.

"Will, stop it!" she screamed, but he acted like he didn't hear her.

"Will!"

Daddy dropped his belt and shifted his stick to his right hand.

"Will."

The stick came down hard across Rick's neck. His head hit the floor, and he was quiet. Daddy raised the stick again, then everything stopped. He stood there, his stick poised like a saber. Mother's eyes were big. Her hands were cupped over her mouth, like she was drinking from them. Rick was wet with pee. His face looked like he was crying, but he wasn't. It was very quiet. I thought we were going to stay that way forever. Then Mother ran and snatched Rick up and shook him.

"Breathe, damn you! Breathe!" she screamed. Then she hugged him to her and broke down and cried.

Rick's back and legs were crisscrossed with long welts that were getting redder and redder. I ran to Mother and grabbed her leg and cried into her skirt. She stepped toward Daddy, and I moved back. He was still standing there with the stick above his head. Mother moved right up to him, until she was standing right under the stick. Tears were streaming down her face, and she was gritting her teeth so hard that I could hear them grinding together.

"God *damn* you, Will Turnbolt!" she screamed. "God *damn* you!"

" 'O Lord, rebuke me not in thine anger, neither chasten me in thy hot displeasure. Have mercy upon me, O Lord, for I am weak. O Lord, heal me, for my bones are vexed. My soul is also sore vexed. But thou, O Lord, how long? Return, O Lord, deliver my soul. Oh, save me for thy mercies' sake. For in death there is no remembrance of thee. In the grave who shall give thee thanks? I am weary with my groaning. All the night make I my bed to swim. I water my couch with my tears. Mine eye is consumed because of grief. It waxeth old because of all mine enemies. Depart from me, all ye workers of iniquity, for the Lord hath heard the voice of my weeping . . .' "

Brother Haskell wept as he read the psalm. He stumbled over the words, pausing again and again to wipe the tears from his eyes. Once he pulled the white handkerchief from his breast pocket and blew his nose. There was weeping all around me. Gran had taken off her glasses and was crying into a flowered handkerchief. Mother was sobbing softly. Her tears glided down her face and dropped on Cherry Ann's frilly pink dress, but Cherry Ann still slept soundly on Mother's lap. Belinda stood in the space between the pews, peering over the back of the pew in front of her. She would look around at me, tears and questions in her eyes, but I couldn't look back at her. The small gray casket and the spray of red roses were a watery blur before me. The casket top was open. I couldn't see Rick, but I knew he was in there.

Harley and Ellen sat at one end of our pew, and Jim Bob, Virgie and Joe George at the other. In the row behind us were the Allisons. Bill Allison sat behind me, and the odor of the mothballs he'd taken his suit out of was even stronger than the sickeningly sweet scent of all the flowers that were arranged on tall stands at each end of the casket.

I'd never seen so many people in church before. The windows were open wide, but it was very hot, anyway, and many of the women cooled themselves with cardboard fans with the picture of Jesus praying that were always stuck in the songbook racks on the backs of the pews.

> *A-bide with me: fast falls the e-ven-tide;*
> *The dark-ness deep-ens; Lord, with me a-bide:*
> *When oth-er help-ers fail, and com-forts flee,*
> *Help of the help-less, O a-bide with me!*

"I don't know what the Lord had in mind when he took Richard Henry Turnbolt," Brother Haskell said. "He was a little boy, hardly big enough to sin. He wasn't yet to the age of accountability. But the Lord must have seen in that small body there a means to work his will, and he used it. What was the Lord's will? Why did Richard Henry Turnbolt die to accomplish it? Our souls are fallen and cannot compre-

hend. We grieve because a child has died. Yet we know
that death in the Lord—and children always die in
the Lord—is not the end, but the beginning of a far,
far better life that will never end! We miss him because he is small and beautiful and we love him. But,
brothers and sisters, it's just for a little while! We are
going to see Richard Henry Turnbolt in glory, by and
by! The Lord sees even the sparrows that fall out of
the air. How much more closely he must be looking
out for Richard Henry Turnbolt!

"As for him that committed this foul deed, what is
to be said for him? That he is to be hated? No. That
he is to be despised? No. 'To me belongeth vengeance
and recompence,' saith the Lord. 'Their foot shall slide
in due time, for the day of their calamity is at hand,
and the things that shall come upon them make haste.'
Don't be angry, brothers and sisters! Don't be afraid!
The Lord will take care of things!"

Then he prayed.

> We shall reach the riv-er side,
> Some sweet day, some sweet day;
> We shall cross the storm-y tide,
> Some sweet day, some sweet day.
> We shall press the sands of gold,
> While before our eyes un-fold
> Heav-en's splen-dor yet un-told,
> Some sweet day, some sweet day.

While the choir sang, we started out of the pews for
our last look at Rick. Harley and Ellen moved aside
and let Mother and Gran go ahead of them. Then
Ellen grabbed Belinda's hand and Harley grabbed
mine and walked us to the casket. Harley picked me
up and held me so I could look in. Rick was dressed

in the little blue sailor suit and the sandals that Gran
had brought him from Comanche. His hair was
brushed into the long curl down the middle of his
head that Mother used to make when she dressed him
up, and his hands lay loosely open on his belly. He
looked like he was asleep. Mother reached into the
casket and squeezed his hand, then turned away.

Bill Allison was standing there. "Lacy," he said, "if
you'd let me, I'd put this in with him."

"All right, Bill," she said.

He laid a rabbit's foot in Rick's hand.

> *We shall meet our loved and own,*
> *Some sweet day, some sweet day;*
> *Gath-ering round the great white throne,*
> *Some sweet day, some sweet day.*
> *By the tree of life so fair,*
> *Joy and rap-ture ev-'ry-where,*
> *O, the bliss of o-ver there!*
> *Some sweet day, some sweet day.*

The long, black funeral-home car was very hot when
we got in, although all the windows were down. Cherry
Ann woke up and started crying. Mother rocked back
and forth in the seat, trying to quiet her.

"We should have taken Virgie up on her offer to
stay home with her," Gran said.

Mother shook her head. "Someday it's going to be
important to her to know she was here," she said.

Belinda stood on the back seat. I was on my knees
beside her, looking through the back window at all
the cars following us up the hill to the cemetery. The
hearse and our car went on through the cemetery
gate and moved slowly among the tombstones to the
green awning that had been stretched above the hole

where we were going to put Rick. The other cars stopped alongside the road, and the people piled out of them and tramped up the gentle rise to the gate.

Brother Haskell stood, Bible clasped to breast, at the head of the grave while Harley and Jim Bob carried Rick's casket from the hearse and laid it on the two poles that had been laid across the hole. They stepped back with us then, and Jim Bob put his arm around Mother's shoulders. She had handed Cherry Ann to Virgie, and Virgie was jiggling her up and down in her arms. Cherry Ann gurgled.

" 'Let not your heart be troubled,' " Brother Haskell read. " 'Ye believe in God, believe also in me. In my Father's house are many mansions. If it were not so, I would have told you. I go to prepare a place for you. And if I go and prepare a place for you, I will come again, and receive you unto myself, that where I am, there ye may be also.' "

And he prayed. The scalloped edges of the awning popped like small flags in the breeze.

Harley and Jim Bob and Bill and one of the men from the funeral home passed two ropes under Rick's casket and lifted it, and another man from the funeral home moved the poles away from the hole. The men lowered the casket, then yanked the ropes out from under it. Harley grabbed the shovel that was sticking up in the mound of dirt next to the hole and held it out to Mother.

She shook her head. "The man of the family ought to be first," she said, and pointed to me.

Harley handed me the shovel. "All right, son," he said. "Do you know what to do?"

"Yes."

I carried the shovel to the dirt pile, filled it as heavy as I could lift, and threw the dirt into the hole.

" 'The Lord is my shepherd,' " Brother Haskell said. " 'I shall not want.' "

I handed the shovel back to Harley, and he picked up some dirt and helped Mother carry it.

" 'He maketh me to lie down in green pastures. He leadeth me beside the still waters.' "

Then Gran.

" 'He restoreth my soul. He leadeth me in the paths of righteousness for his name's sake.' "

Then Harley.

" 'Yea, though I walk through the valley of the shadow of death, I will fear no evil, for thou art with me. Thy rod and thy staff they comfort me.' "

Then Jim Bob.

" 'Thou preparest a table before me in the presence of mine enemies. Thou anointest my head with oil. My cup runneth over.' "

Then Bill.

" 'Surely goodness and mercy shall follow me all the days of my life, and I will dwell in the house of the Lord for ever.' "

We were about to get back into the funeral-home car when I saw him standing in the shade of a big cedar among the tombstones. A man wearing a gun was with him, and Daddy looked very lonesome.

We were moving. I didn't know why, or exactly where, but we were. All our furniture and stuff was out in the front yard, and people were driving up in cars and pickups and wagons, and Mother and Gran were selling it for whatever they were offered, and the people were hauling it off. By sundown, there was nothing left but a couple of broken-down chairs and one book end and a few old shoes and books and stuff. Gran just gathered them all up and took them out to the trash pile and set fire to them.

We rattled like marbles in that empty house. Mother and Gran moved around, folding clothes and putting them in suitcases and cardboard boxes and Gran's old trunk. Their footsteps echoed through the rooms. Belinda followed them around, talking to them and getting in their way. Cherry Ann was asleep in a wash-tub with some quilts in it. The house seemed darker with everything gone. The bare light-bulbs dangling from the ceilings looked dimmer than before, and the shadows of all of us were bigger and darker than I remembered them being. The wallpaper was faded and spotted with soot and water rings. The linoleum was cracked and broken. I'd never noticed these things before. The house was old and worn-out. I was glad we were leaving it. I wished we were already gone.

"Gate, come help us pack the car," Mother said. "Belinda can watch the baby."

"Okay."

Gran's car was parked under the tree next to the back door. She was poking around inside the trunk with a flashlight.

"I think the suitcases and some of the boxes will fit in here, Lacy," she said. "The rest can go on top."

"Yeah, but if we tie the baby bed on the back, we can't open the trunk," Mother said.

"I know. We'll just have to wear the same clothes until we get there. Cherry Ann's diapers can go in the front seat with us."

"Well, okay. God, I dread this."

"So do I. But we have to do what we have to do, so we might as well get started."

We lifted and pulled and shoved. Gran's old trunk was the hardest part. It had to go between the seats, and since it was a two-door car, it was hard to get the thing in. I got inside the car and pulled on the handle, and Mother and Gran shoved and turned the trunk every which a way until we finally got it in. The top of the trunk was almost level with the back seat, so we spread quilts over it all and made a pretty cozy-looking pallet.

I climbed to the top of the car, onto the rack that Pearly White had given us, and Mother and Gran heaved boxes and bundles up to me. I piled them the best I could, covered the whole thing with a sheet, and tied it down with some cotton rope. Then we tied the two spare tires on the front, and the pieces of Cherry Ann's bed on the back.

"What's left?" Gran asked, poking the flashlight around in the darkness.

"Just the ironing board," Mother said.

"Oh, Lordy! Where are we going to put that?"

"Don't worry. We'll make it," Mother said. "We're not licked yet."

"How about the running board?" I asked.

"Well, we couldn't open the door . . ." Gran said.

"We could open one door," Mother said. "We're lucky we won't have to climb through the windows."

Cherry Ann let out a yell. Mother went into the house to check on her, and Gran and I worked on the ironing board.

"How far is it to El Paso?" I asked.

"I don't know. Three days. Maybe a little longer. There. One more knot ought to do it, honey."

"Okay. I'm finished."

"Let's check it over."

We walked around the car, and Gran flashed the light around over all the ropes and knots.

"It's sure loaded, isn't it?" she said.

"Yeah. Hope it all stays on."

"It will. Let's go in."

Mother was changing Cherry Ann's diaper on the kitchen drainboard. She chuckled while Mother sprinkled the talcum powder on her.

"We're through," Gran said.

"Good. Get the kids in the car while I finish up here. I don't want to stay around here any longer than we have to."

Belinda was sitting on the living room floor, staring at the wall. "I want to go to bed," she said.

"Too bad," I said. "There's no bed here."

"Come on, honey," Gran said, picking her up. "There's a nice pallet in the car. Will you turn out the lights, Lacy? I don't want to come back."

"Yes, I'll be right out."

Gran laid Belinda on the pallet and put a pillow under her head, then scooted under the steering wheel and across the front seat.

"Can I sit in the front for a while?" I asked.

"Sure, honey." She patted the seat beside her.

We watched the light go out in the living room, and then in the kitchen. Belinda sat up.

"Are we moving now?" she asked.

"Yes, just as soon as your mother gets here," Gran said.

"When are we coming back?"

"Oh, I don't know. Someday. Maybe."

Mother came down the steps and handed Cherry Ann through the window to Gran and got in and started the engine. The lights flicked on.

"Everybody set?" Mother asked.

"I think so," Gran said. "How's the gas?"

"Full. I had it filled when Pearly put the rack on. He gave it to us out of his own gas stamps."

"That was mighty nice of him," Gran said. "There are lots of good people in this world."

Mother backed the car into the street and turned it toward town. Lights were still on in some of the houses. People were sitting on their front porches, getting the breeze. They looked at us when we went by. Gran waved at some. Nobody was downtown. Everything was closed. Small bulbs burned in some of the stores, making their ordinary merchandise look eerie. Others were dark, and our headlights flashed back at us through their black windows. A light was burning behind a drawn shade above the drugstore. Mother turned and drove by the burned-out bank and the Helpy-Selfy. Soon we passed the last house, stopped, and turned onto the highway. I turned and grinned at Belinda. I could barely see her through the darkness.

"We're on our way!" I said.

She nodded. She was sleepy. Everybody was quiet. Mother hunched over the steering wheel, looking straight ahead, too. The car wasn't as crowded as I thought it would be. The diaper bag and the Thermos jug were on the floor. The flashlight and the map were on the dashboard. That was all. The headlights cut a short yellow path ahead of us. A cottontail crossed it. A nighthawk crossed it. Two headlights met us, dimmed, moved past. Johnson grass and sunflowers waved lazily in the edge of the light. There were fence posts, bridge rails, a light in a farmhouse window. The motor hummed. The dashboard lights shined on Cherry Ann's sleeping face. She had her thumb in her mouth. I wanted to talk.

"How far are we going tonight?" I asked.

"Shh! You'll wake the kids up!" Gran whispered.

"How far?" I whispered.

"Far enough to find a tourist camp and put these kids to bed."

"How far is that?"

"We'll see. Dublin, maybe."

"That's not far!"

"Shh!"

The motor hummed. I got stiff. I shifted around.

"You want to get in the back?" Gran whispered.

"No."

"You can if you want to."

"I don't want to."

I saw the lights of Dublin. I sat up straight to get a better look. Mother slowed the car as we started through town.

"There's one," Gran said, pointing to a row of white cabins.

"No vacancy," Mother said.

"What does that mean?" I asked.

"They're all filled up. No more room. There's another one."

"No vacancy," Gran said.

"Another one."

"No vacancy."

"We'll try Comanche," Mother said.

We tried Comanche and Blanket and Early and Brownwood and Bangs. Everywhere there were tourist camps and cars. Nowhere was there a vacancy.

"Get up, birthday boy!"

Gran was standing by the bed, grinning. Mother was with her, holding Cherry Ann.

"Wake up, kids," Gran said. "It's Gate's birthday!"

Belinda stirred beside me. She rubbed her eyes and stretched, and Mother and Gran sang the birthday song. When they moved aside, I saw a chocolate covered doughnut on the dresser. One lighted candle was stuck in it.

"They didn't have any birthday cake at the cafe," Mother said, "but the waitress did the best she could. Come make a wish."

There were two little somethings wrapped up in Kleenex, one on each side of the doughnut. I shut my eyes and wished that our trip was over and we were there. I blew, and Mother and Gran clapped their hands.

"Open your presents, Gate," Mother said.

They were two fifty-cent pieces.

"That's a whole dollar," Gran said. "You can buy your own present when we get to El Paso. Something to start a new life with."

We went to the tourist camp cafe and ate breakfast.

I'd never been to a cafe before. There was a shiny
counter with stools and a lot of tables. It was full of
soldiers and sailors and women and kids. Everybody
was talking pretty loud. A woman in a white dress
came over to our table.

"Did you hear the news?" she asked.

"We just got up," Gran said. "What news?"

"The Japs have surrendered!"

"You don't mean it!"

"Yep, it's in all the papers. The war's over!"

Mother and Gran talked about the war and the Japs
and General MacArthur all through breakfast. Gran
bought a newspaper and read to us about it all after
we got on the road. Mother and Gran were real happy
about it for a while, but then Gran quit reading and
folded the paper and stuck it under the seat. She sat
there staring ahead at the highway, and then she had
tears in her eyes.

"If only it had come sooner," she said.

"Yes, but it didn't," Mother said. "It just didn't.
Let's don't talk about it any more."

Gran wiped her eyes and looked at us in the back
seat. "Well, kids," she said. "Are you enjoying the
trip?"

"Yes."

"Want me to tell you about where we're going?"

"Yes."

"It's in the high mountains, far to the west. There
are lots of horses and cows and cowboys and Mexi-
cans, and they have a school, and Belinda's going to
be in the first grade, and Gate's going to be in the
third grade, and I'm going to be a teacher. I know a
song about it. Want me to sing it?"

"Yeah!" Belinda said. "Sing."

"Okay! Here goes! One! Two! Three! Lacy, you join in."

> *Oh, give me a home, where the buf-fa-lo roam,*
> *Where the deer and the an-te-lope play,*
> *Where sel-dom is heard a dis-cour-ag-ing word,*
> *And the skies are not clou-dy all day.*

Mother joined in on the chorus, and pretty soon everybody was laughing and carrying on and having a good time. Gran told us stories and read us Burma-Shave signs and asked us riddles and told us the names of the towns we went through. There were hills of bare whitish rock and cactus and scrubby little dark green bushes. There was the sun, always shimmering on the highway ahead of us, always playing tricks, making us see lakes and rivers that weren't there. There were detours and machines and dust and men waving red flags at us. There were filling stations and toilets and the smell of gas and men asking us where we were from and where we were going. There was sweat, and Cherry Ann crying. There was Mother, hunched over the steering wheel, squinting through her shades into the sun, and Gran, looking at the map. There were tourist camps and cafes and NO VACANCY signs. There was supper and more highway and a long black train full of soldiers and more ice in the Thermos and a diaper change beside the road and the stink of dirty diapers in the front seat and cars with big, round air coolers in their windows and a purple-and-yellow-and-orange-and-green sundown, and finally, there was a bed and sleep.

The highway stretched ahead of us like an endless

blue ribbon across an endless brown table. There were no houses, no animals, no people. Then they were there, like huge windmill towers. Their stink came to meet us.

"Oil derricks," Gran said. "Black gold. Stinks to high heaven, doesn't it?"

"I wish some of that stink belonged to us," Mother said. "It'd probably smell pretty good, then."

Everything was sun and hot metal, pipe and sheet iron and derricks and trucks and men in shiny steel hats and sheds and pumps working up and down like crazy hobby-horses and bare black ground and pools of dirty, stinking stuff. Then there was more sand and brush and derricks and oil. There was an air base with acres and acres of shiny bombers, lined up row on row, like they were growing in a field. We stopped and watched one come in for a landing.

"Well, boys," Gran said, watching it. "I guess you'll all be going home soon."

The sun was setting when we passed through Pecos. The desert was still before us, but off in the distance was a line of blue mountains.

"Well, kids, that's where we're going," Gran said.

"Yes, right through them," Mother said. "They scare me to death, just looking at them. I've never driven in mountains before."

"I'm not worried, Lacy. You're a good driver."

"Famous last words! Well, here goes!"

The mountains were farther away than they looked, and it was dark long before we got to them. Then the road narrowed and started winding, and we were climbing through the blackest blackness I'd ever seen. There were no houses, no towns, no cars, no lights.

Just the road and its black center stripe and the little reflectors on the guard posts, warning us of curves and cliffs. I kept imagining that the lights were getting dimmer, and I wondered what we would do if they went out. Everyone was awake, but it was very quiet. Belinda and I sat bolt upright in the back seat. Cherry Ann lay quietly in Gran's lap. My heart was in my throat. I kept wondering if that road really ended anywhere or just kept going on and on through the blackness.

Your face has almost faded from my mind, my father, into the long silence. But I'll cut a rose with this old bone-handled knife and lay it on the dark earth that covers you.

William Lafayette Turnbolt, prominent Carson County farmer and civic leader, died at 4:15 p.m. yesterday at Grayson Memorial Hospital. He was 54.

Mr. Turnbolt, formerly of Darlington, Tex., moved to Calloway in 1952, shortly after his marriage to Mrs. Miriam Colson, widow of the late G. H. Colson and owner of Colson Farms. He entered immediately into community life and over the years served terms as president of the Calloway Lions Club, worshipful master of Carson Lodge No. 769, F&AM, deacon of First Baptist Church, and advisor to the Carson County 4-H Club. He was a director of the Farmers & Merchants State Bank from 1955 until his death. He served in the Army during World War II.

Survivors include his widow, two sons, Robert and William Jr., both students at the University of Texas at Austin; a daughter, Cynthia, a sophomore at Carson County High School, and other children by previous marriages.

The funeral will be at First Baptist Church at 10 a.m. Friday, with burial in Crestview Cemetery. The body may be viewed at Johnson & Bennett Funeral Home after 2 p.m. tomorrow.

Expressions of sympathy may take the form of contributions to the First Baptist Church organ fund.

ABOUT THE AUTHOR

BRYAN WOOLLEY was born in Texas in 1937 and grew
up in Fort Davis, a small mountain town west of the
Pecos. He received most of his education from the
people who live there, and the rest at the University
of Texas at El Paso, Texas Christian University and
Harvard. He is a journalist whose career has included
sojourns at the El Paso *Times*, the Tulsa bureau of
The Associated Press and the Anniston *Star* in
Alabama. He is at present a writer for the Louisville
Courier-Journal and Louisville *Times Magazine.*